PRAISE FOR DORTHE NORS

"The darkly comic Danish writer [Dorthe Nors] is at her wiliest when she's most direct. . . . Beneath the cool minimalism roils maximalist outrage."　　　　　　　—*The New York Times*

"Dorthe Nors covers the emotional spectrum . . . finding as much material in the comedy of rejection as in its humiliations and heartbreak."　　　　　　　—*The Wall Street Journal*

"Spare and sublime. Dorthe Nors knows how to capture the smallest moments and sculpt them into the unforgettable."
—*O, The Oprah Magazine*

"Dorthe Nors is a writer of moments—quiet, raw portraits of existential meditation, at times dyspeptic, but never unsympathetic."
—*The Paris Review*

"In flowing and absorbing prose, Nors illustrates . . . how it might be possible for anyone to overcome immense loneliness and make a connection."　　　　　　　—*The New Yorker*

"Danish sensation Dorthe Nors . . . evoke[s] the weirdness and wonder of relating in the digital age."　　　　　　　—*Vogue*

"Dorthe Nors focus[es] on ordinary occurrences . . . and then twist[s] them into brilliantly slanted cautionary tales about desire, romance, deception, and dread."　　　　　　　—*ELLE*

"Nors's writing is by turns witty, gut wrenching, stark and lyrical. . . . That she achieves all this while experimenting with form is something of an impossible feat."
—*Los Angeles Times*

WILD
SWIMS

WILD SWIMS

STORIES

DORTHE NORS

TRANSLATED FROM THE DANISH BY MISHA HOEKSTRA

GRAYWOLF PRESS

Wild Swims was first published as *Kort Over Canada* by Gyldendal in Denmark, 2018. First published in English by Pushkin Press in 2020.

Published by agreement with Ahlander Agency.

"The Freezer Chest" appeared in the *New Yorker*. "Hygge" appeared in Longreads.com and in *Harper's Magazine*. "By Sydvest Station" appeared in Novelleforlaget and in *Tin House*. "In a Deer Stand" appeared in *The Dark Blue Winter Overcoat & Other Stories* (ed. Sjón and Ted Hodgkinson, Pushkin Press) and in *A Public Space*. "Sun Dogs" appeared on newyorker.com.

This publication is made possible, in part, by the voters of Minnesota through a Minnesota State Arts Board Operating Support grant, thanks to a legislative appropriation from the arts and cultural heritage fund. Significant support has also been provided by Target Foundation, the McKnight Foundation, the Lannan Foundation, the Amazon Literary Partnership, and other generous contributions from foundations, corporations, and individuals. To these organizations and individuals we offer our heartfelt thanks.

The author gratefully acknowledges the Danish Arts Council and its Committee for Literary Project Funding and the Danish Arts Agency for support in the writing and translation of this book—and to Hald Hovedgaard for a writing residency.

DANISH ARTS FOUNDATION

Published by Graywolf Press
250 Third Avenue North, Suite 600
Minneapolis, Minnesota 55401

www.graywolfpress.org

Published in the United States of America

ISBN 978-1-64445-043-7

2 4 6 8 9 7 5 3 1
First Graywolf Printing, 2021

Library of Congress Control Number: 2020937595

Cover design and art: Kimberly Glyder

CONTENTS

You can always withdraw
a little bit further

IN A DEER STAND

IT'S A QUESTION OF TIME. SOONER OR LATER, SOME-body will show up. Even dirt tracks like these can't stay deserted forever. The farm he passed when he entered the area must be inhabited. The people who live there must go for walks some-times. And the deer stand is probably the farmer's, and it's just a question of time before it starts raining. The vegetation on the ground is dry. Some twiggy bushes, some heather too. To the right, a thicket; to the left, the start of a tree plantation. The dirt road must go in there for a reason, so someone comes here now and then. Take him, for instance, *he* came this way. Just yesterday, even if it feels longer. The circumstances make it feel longer. It's likely that his ankle's broken, though it's also possible that it's just a sprain. The pain isn't constant. There *is* some swelling. Now he sits here and he has no phone. She must be in pieces back home. He can imagine it. Walking around with his phone in her hand, out in the utility room. She's standing there with it in her hand. She curses him for not taking it. He supposes the police will be involved soon. Maybe they already have been for some time now. It's probably been on the local radio; that he's forty-seven, that he drives a BMW, that he left home in a depressed state. He can't bear the thought of them saying those last words. She just wasn't supposed to win every battle.

Last night there was screeching in the forest. Some owls, foxes perhaps. Someone has seen wolves out here, and no doubt Lisette has come by the house. Lisette's probably sitting on the couch with her wide eyes, eating it all up. He's so tired. His clothes are damp, and last night he froze something terrible. There are black birds overhead, rooks he thinks, and she's pacing around in the yard, restless. He painted the eaves last spring. It's a nice house, but she wants to sell it now. He really likes the house, but now she wants something else. When she wants something else, there's nothing he can do. As recently as the day before yesterday, he had an urge to call his brother, but he's lost that battle. Lisette's welcome to visit. Lisette often stands in their kitchen-dining area and calls up her network. Lisette's got a big network, but mostly she hangs out with his. And in principle, he's only got the kids left. It's a long time since she took part in the gatherings on his side of the family. There's something wrong with his parents, she says. Something wrong with his brother's kids, his brother's girlfriend, and especially his brother. She says that his brother sows discord. That's because his brother once told him he ought to get divorced. And because he loses all battles, he went straight home and told her: "My brother thinks I should get divorced." So this isn't the first time he's driven out to some forest. He's done it a fair amount over the years. Sometimes to call up his folks on the sly, or his brother. He also calls them when he's down washing the car.

He's sitting in a deer stand, and something's happened to the light. A mist is rising. It creeps toward him across the crowberry bushes. Which means that evening is closing in again. He wanted to be alone, so that's what he is now. He stepped on a tussock wrong, in the strip between the wheel ruts, some seventy-five yards from the deer stand. First the pain, then off with the sock. Did he shout for someone? Well, he shouted a bit the first hour, then darkness began to descend and he set about reaching the deer stand.

He adds up the distances between towns. It must be about seventy-nine miles home. That's how far he is from the utility room, where she's standing and staring at his phone, though no doubt Lisette's there. Lisette's playing the role of comforter, co-conspirator, and slave, yes, Lisette's her slave too, but a slave with privileges. While he heard something shrieking in the forest last night. Probably a fox, but wolves have been sighted here too. The hunters set up game cameras to get a glimpse of the animals they hope to shoot. Or else it's farmers wanting photos of whatever's eating their turnips, usually red deer, he supposes. Then one morning this wolf is standing there, staring straight into the camera. He's seen it in the newspaper, but wolves can't climb, and it's just a question of time before she sits down next to the washing machine. Her hands cupped over her knees, and he hasn't seen her cry in years. She didn't cry when her mother died. Her face can clap shut over a feeling like the lid of a freezer over stick insects. He had some in eighth grade, in a terrarium, stick insects. They weren't much fun, and then his biology teacher said that putting them in the freezer would kill them. He peered at the insects for a long time before he placed them in the freezer. They stood there rocking, looking stalklike. When he took the terrarium out the next day, they stood there stiff. They didn't suffer, he supposed. Thinking back on them now, they looked like someone who's achieved complete control over a stage illusion—and she's been successful that way too. Maybe she doesn't have feelings at all. She's got lots of hobbies, but it isn't clear that she has feelings. He has the distinct sense that Lisette's standing in the kitchen area at this very moment. Lisette sits in the bedroom on the edge of the bed, she's there for the kids' graduation parties, she joins them on vacation, and for several years she drove their daughter to handball. Lisette's got short legs and a driver's license, and by now the police must have been brought in. It's been more than a day since he drove off. In a depressed state of mind, though that's not true. He just wanted the feeling of winning, and now he has a view of a landscape at dusk. His trousers are green from moss and something else, extending high up his legs. The boards he's sitting on have been attacked by algae. If she saw this sort of algae on the patio, she'd have him fetch the poison. What *hasn't* he done on that house? And now she wants to move into something smaller, though it'd be good to have an extra room. "An extra room?" he asked. "For Lisette," she replied, and then he took the car and left his phone behind. His family's grown used to his absence, and besides, he isn't the same any more. Something has clapped shut over him. First she won all the battles, then he positioned himself squarely on her side. In that way, he stopped losing, and she tired of scrutinizing him. That was the logic, but now he's sitting here. A mist has risen, the night will be cold, and a wolf has been sighted.

SUN DOGS

IT'S A LONG TIME AGO NOW, BUT ONCE I LIVED IN A cabin in Norway. It was Olav who mentioned the place to me, at the start of our relationship. He told me it had been the summer cottage of the Norwegian author Knut Terje Aasbakken. Now it was a writer's retreat, and a narrow lane led up to it from the village Olav came from. As a boy, he'd go up there sometimes to spy on the writers who lived there. They seemed so secretive, he said, and dove into me.

The spring that our relationship began to get complicated, Olav invited me to the King's Garden. I didn't take it lightly, I begged, but he would not relent. As July drew on I became a wisp, and a friend suggested I go away somewhere. So it was I remembered Aasbakken's cabin. The one in Norway, on a mountainside, in a forest.

I applied, got the cabin, left at the beginning of September. A woman from the general store drove me up from the village. She talked about the area as we crept up the mountain in her little Golf. On the way we passed the community center. She said it was customary for whoever lived in the cabin to give a reading at the center. I gazed down on the river in the valley, and then she dropped me off with a key to the woodshed.

Evenings, I would take a chair out in front of the cabin and try to stay in it till I was shaking from the cold. In the mornings, I read over the notes I'd brought along, wrote nothing.

Late in the day I would take a walk, usually on the path down to the village. I read the nameplates on the doors I passed, and then one day I found myself at a standstill in front of the community center notice board. BUNADS, the heading read, and under it the name of Olav's mother. She was called Halldis and taught the locals how to sew their own folk costumes.

The days lasted an eternity, and at night the cold moved in. I walked around Aasbakken's house and picked paint from the cabinet doors. Out in the forest the mushrooms poked up, and it was impossible to escape the reading event at the community center. The chair of the library club came by several times and pressed. One evening in October, I positioned myself against a large loom-woven tapestry, read aloud and talked. During the coffee break, a woman with short dark hair and a face with Inuit features came over to me. She said, "I think you've met my son. He lives in Copenhagen." I must have stared. "I've got an article he's written about you," she said. "Who's your son?" I asked, and the answer was obvious.

That was how I became a friend of sorts with Olav's mother, Halldis. We agreed to go on some walks together. Later we also went out riding on her Fjord horses. She talked about the landscape, the kinds of tracks animals left, and how the winter we were entering would feel. We never spoke of Olav. I didn't mention him, and she was private. I had the impression that she was a strong person, but at regular intervals she would worry about whether I'd write about her.

One day in early November, we took the horses out into the forest. When we came to a clearing, I said that the vista there would make for a good opening scene. Then she said, "Yes, that's what I'm so afraid of."

She looked at her hands grasping the reins, and I thought of Olav, his face and hers, and that might have been the day she invited me home for coffee. In any case, I remember that we let the horses loose in the pasture and sat in the kitchen. There were pictures of Olav and his wife on the bulletin board, and I'm sure that I gave Halldis a hug when I left. At least I remember that something felt difficult about the parting.

Despite the awkwardness in our relationship, we kept seeing each other. One day when we were in the kitchen after a hike, Olav's father came in. He was reluctant to sit down at the table, as we probably didn't want to be disturbed. Halldis found him a coffee cup, and of course he was disturbing us. I recall him saying on several occasions that he didn't care for well-educated people. He was a carpenter, Olav's father. Said that the hand's labor was important and pointed to the table. I praised the table, and then I had to go and see his workshop.

We walked out to it, all three of us, and what I remember most clearly about the room was that he'd stuck up a photo of a naked woman with a thumbtack. He'd pinned her up over the door to the room where Halldis worked on her costumes. That meant that Halldis had to walk under the naked woman anytime she went in to do her sewing. You never know about other people's relationships, but I thought to myself that it was their marriage Halldis didn't want me to write about. It seemed complicated to me, though I think it seemed healthy to her. Every day she passed beneath the naked woman who hung over the door with her legs slightly spread, and had hung there so long that Halldis no longer noticed her. She was no doubt thinking of her son in Copenhagen. His wife was beautiful and industrious. He himself interviewed famous authors. And now one of them was living in Aasbakken's cabin.

The cabin had no phone, so of course I ended up getting a letter. I have it still. He was angry, Olav. "I wouldn't have thought it of you," he wrote.

In that sense, he wasn't like his mother, and I can recall another time we rode out together. It was a clear fall morning, and she mounted easily. On the outward part of our route, we rode past a lake. To me, Norwegian lakes feel bottomless, the landscape unknowable. Such uncertainty must leave its mark on the locals, I thought. Later we went in among the trees, where it smelled of fungus and rot. When we came to the clearing, I said, again, "This scene would lend itself to a story," and I pointed at the animal paths crisscrossing the terrain. "That's also what I'm afraid of," she said. "What are you afraid of?" I asked, and she replied, as always, that she was afraid I would write about her.

As we rode on, we talked about how the forest looked lovely in its decay. I told her she reminded me of an Inuit in some ways, and that Olav must have gotten his features from her. She smiled at that, and there were birds of prey aloft, and moss upon the massive trunks of spruce. "Look over there, the moss," she said, and I drank in everything I saw.

But then one day, when we were drinking coffee in the kitchen and her husband came in, wanting attention, she actually began to tell a story. She looked at Olav's father, asked him, "Do I dare to tell this?" and he said, "Yes, just tell it."

At first I thought she asked him whether she should tell the story because it was his, or because he decided which stories could be told in their relationship. In any case she began telling it, and at regular intervals she'd put a hand over her mouth. "No, I don't know if I dare," she said, glancing from her husband down into her cup. "You really don't have to," I said.

The story she was telling concerned her cousin who had been married to a bad man. Then he died, and it wasn't until then that the cousin discovered just how bad he'd been. It came out in certain letters found with the estate. "But you mustn't write this story," she said, "that's what I'm scared of." I said that she shouldn't be worried. "Your cousin's husband wasn't so out of the ordinary." She asked, did I know such men? I said that now and then I ran into one. She asked if I wrote about them. "Sometimes," I said.

I have the impression that during the time we spent together, she managed to read my books. She mentioned one in particular during a hike. It had become winter, we were in the forest, and the surroundings creaked with snow and ice. She'd read the book but didn't quite know what to think of it. She found the indecisiveness of the female protagonist especially hard to bear.

We crawled over an old stone wall. The sun was shining, my eyes hurt from all the whiteness, and recently I had seen an old photo from the gold-mining town of Yellowknife, near the Arctic Circle. It was a picture of an Inuit and then the sun, and it wasn't alone. It had company. It's an optical phenomenon—the sun's light is refracted by ice crystals and two bright points appear, one on either side. Under the picture it said that the sun had been joined by its rivals, the ones that in the language of the prairie were called *sun dogs*. As she stood there, Halldis, with her hood covering her ears, she could have been taken for such a figure. Strong in profile, yet still fragile.

"What exactly are you afraid I'm going to write about?" I asked her then. "I don't know," she said.

She stood there and the light went right through her, that's the way I remember it. How the sun caused her physical form to cease. On the broad white expanse she cast a sharp shadow and I stood opposite her, not alone.

"Halldis?" I said.

She tugged at her mittens, nodded.

HYGGE

THEN WE WERE SITTING THERE, LILLY AND ME, AND she had made coffee and baked one of those chocolate cakes that are soft in the middle. That afternoon she'd also vacuumed and cleared the dead leaves off the windowsills. The budgie was no longer chattering in its cage but had been put to rest under a dish towel, and on the TV there was some show we could guess along with. When I'd come by in the afternoon, it hadn't been so nice. We'd had a falling-out about her behavior, about the way she'd act up when we were at the senior club, her jealousy and her sweetness, which just seemed vulgar. And then she'd said that business about my face—that she didn't like it. "You and your big professor mug," she'd said, and the floor in the bathroom had been littered with laundry. She hadn't made the bed either, and there was that sweetish smell of urine. I know that smell from Aunt Clara's, back when she could no longer see and fumbled around and knocked everything over, especially herself. It was as if something dead had taken up permanent residence in her cells, and now it oozed out during her trips to the toilet. It settled into the wallpaper, and the odor was there when we would sit down to enjoy the fruit drink that I'd mix up out in her kitchen. Those long afternoons with flat fruit drink, peppermint candies, and Aunt Clara, who no longer fit her teeth. There are some things you never forget. The way we sang from the songbook, for instance, and her transcriptions of the King's speeches on New Year's Eve, and I've never understood why Aunt Clara's loneliness required my involvement. I was just a boy, and while I sat there and had King Frederik's words placed in my mouth, I suppose my folks were at the movie theater. "You're so clever in school," they'd say. "That sort of thing needs stimulation," they'd say, and then Aunt Clara would be there with her fingers on my neck, the bowl of sugar cubes up in my face: "Take one, my boy, take two, eat!"

But now she'd made coffee, Lilly had, she'd made coffee and she'd covered the budgie and taken out the nice cups. There wasn't any more talk about my face. Her little hand was up in my hair, inside the waist of my trousers, and she wanted to get hold of my hand, "Because now we we're going to have us a cozy time and not talk any more about it."

It was the Pharmacist who got me into the club, claiming we'd play chess, but as a bachelor I had to place my body at the disposal of all the cast-off women and their expectations. Then I had a sock they needed to see to, then there was something about my collar, then their feet started hurting and they wanted to be driven home. And among the desperate, Lilly stood out. First she tried to latch on to the Pharmacist, but the other women were on him like hyenas around a cadaver. It was his fine beard, she said, and no doubt you can say some good things about Lilly, but those fancy blouses can't cover up what can't be changed. All that frippery, yes, the budgie too, it only drags her down, and then we were sitting there, it was Saturday and the tea lights were lit. She had placed them along the edge of the bookcase, with tinfoil wrapped around the bases so they wouldn't burn down into the laminate. It had happened to her before, that the tea lights had burned into the laminate, and she'd also had them explode. The liquid wax could be as flammable as gasoline, so she felt safer with tapers. The dignified sort. So long as you didn't set them up against the curtains, you could count on them. "They're a bit like you," she giggled, "so orderly and erect," she said, scooting her way off the couch and out into the kitchen, where I could hear her rummaging around. "But if we can just stay awake, the little ones should be fine!" she shouted, and I've often thought that Lilly's someone who could easily fall asleep with a cigarette in her hand. I could see her doing that on the couch, beneath the sun-faded pictures of her relatives. There's one of Lilly hanging there too, from sometime in the '70s. She's got her hair crimped with an iron, the way my students crimped theirs back then. There they would sit, trying to make themselves attractive while I struggled with their sloppy logarithm assignments. That is if they weren't tottering around on those espadrilles that were much too high, as if they'd attached hay bales beneath their feet, good Lord, and their shampoo stank in the classroom. Prostitutes struck me as less manipulative, and more economical, and the last day before Christmas break was the worst. The deep-fried æbleskiver and mulled wine, and we were supposed to talk about the year that had passed. As if the year could do anything else. As if that's not precisely the way time works, and Lilly's also hung up school pictures of her aging offspring. There's something about their faces, something dumplingish and soft. They've had far too much candy, those kids, and now they're living on another side street in the same neighborhood with kids of their own, kids who are also too fat, but that's not something you can tell

Lilly. She doesn't feel anything, most of the time, but it takes nothing at all to make her feel everything, and then she was sidling through the door with a tray. "We're having Baileys with coffee," she said. Baileys and some peppermints she had left over from Christmas. "We're going to have it a little nice," she said, and then she squeezed herself in next to me on the couch, her fingers with the defunct wedding bands, and the jingle of amethyst and other costume jewels dangling from her earlobes. I guess she's harmless enough, it's all just heat, I know that and the Pharmacist says the same, but Baileys tastes of German rest stops and the corner of some party where nothing's happening. Besides, Lilly should be able to tell that I'm more one for whiskey. Or a dry cognac with a cigar. I want to play chess! I'm nobody's pet, and don't think I don't know what she, Clara, has under the sink or out by the electric meter. I know all about the liquor from the corner store. It's starting to pickle her face, to lay her tongue in brine. She can't hide anything from me. I've known her for a dog's age, and I can't be led around by the nose anymore. But it was as we were sitting on the couch, me with her free hand on my trouser knee and her with her eye on the Baileys, that she said, "We're good friends, aren't we? I know I'm stupid," she said, "and it can't be easy for you with all your brains to go around with someone like me," she said. "So can't we just be cozy?" And so we were. We sat there and were cozy, and I can't account for how we got from when she took the last bite of cake to when she was lying there down on the floor, halfway under the coffee table, eyes gawping, mouth too, but even then, when it all was over and done, it looked as if she was forcing me, and I didn't like it.

BY SYDVEST STATION

THEY'RE READY. THEY HAVE A COLLECTION CAN, A BAG with the cancer logo, and two streets by Sydvest Station with an apartment co-op and some rental flats, and Kirsten has no idea what she's in for, just that it'll be exciting to try collecting money for the Cancer Society in a neighborhood like this, while Lina steels herself for the awkwardness of standing so far from home in her white sneakers and rattling the can. She's also tired, and at the same time her head is full of him and what he said. It hurt her, and she's felt tired ever since, like she could fall asleep on her feet. But Kirsten's game, and Lina smiles at her and says that she is too, and then they get started.

At the first building no one answers initially, even though they press all the buttons on the intercom, but it must be the guy on the fifth floor who finally lets them in, as he ends up being the only one who contributes. He gives them twenty kroner, and then they giggle all the way downstairs because it's the first money they've ever collected, but also because they're nervous. Some of the doors make it clear how odd people can be. They put stickers with Rottweilers, Bambi, and Cinderella around their nameplates, which sometimes are galvanized and other times written in ballpoint and stuck up with masking tape. There are also doors that send mixed messages, and the two of them talk about how you never know what awaits you when you knock on someone's door. True enough, Lina thinks to herself, musing that Kirsten for instance doesn't know that he said what he said. In fact nobody knows that he told her that—that her love couldn't be genuine. That no one really loved that way. It was just compensation, he'd said, but she doesn't want to tell Kirsten that. She's certain her reaction would be textbook, and nothing's worse than someone who goes by the book, Lina thinks, saying nothing, and then Kirsten suggests that they start using the decorations on each door to guess what sort of person might answer.

They guess wrong almost every time, but that's what makes it fun, even when some of the people who open the doors are strange. They speak indistinctly, or they answer the door in their PJs, and many of them seem annoyed. One man is grumpy about being woken up on a Sunday morning and he snaps at them. Other places, there's a rustling behind the door. People whisper inside, though everything's audible out on the landing: "Don't open it. I'm sick and tired of all these people asking for money," says a woman behind one door, while at another, a kid comes out and slots some change in the can while Mommy and Daddy look on. They clap and say, "How clever," and Lina thinks that people are weird. Their flats smell intimate, and filth is one thing, but their cleaning solutions seem like something you don't really want to know about either, and "Hello, we're from the Cancer Society, would you like to support our work?"

That's their spiel. But it's not really true. Neither she nor Kirsten has anything to do with the Cancer Society, and personally, she doesn't want to have anything to do with them either. This is all about spending a Sunday with a friend, and since they came up with the business of the door decorations in the second stairwell, Lina's also been feeling like a tourist—plus she supposes that what they're doing is a form of begging. Ringing on strange people's doorbells to demand love and respect, Lina thinks, and in the fifth building she's on the point of remonstrating with a young man who says through the letter slot that he has no money but is a big fan of what they do. She wants to tell him that she isn't doing anything. "All I'm doing is trying to move on after my emotional life went to the dogs, so shove it, motherfucker, you goddamn loser," she thinks of saying—if she were the type to say such things. But she isn't. She knows perfectly well that she's more the type to focus on how sticky the floors seem in some of the flats and how gross it is, and that, despite all the door decoration, people aren't very modest about their lives. That some places stink of medicine and dogs. Even though people aren't allowed to have dogs in apartments like these, and even if they are, they shouldn't be, Lina tells Kirsten, and Kirsten says she glimpsed a fighting dog through the letter slot of the fifth-floor flat in the seventh building, where the tenant, a younger woman, gave them two hundred because, as she put it, "My own life has been affected."

Welcome to the club, Lina thinks, thrusting the can toward Kirsten because it feels like it's begun to stick to her fingers. Welcome to the club, is all I can say, she thinks. But she doesn't say it aloud.

They walk purposefully from building to building, or at least Kirsten does. As for Lina, she's just along for the ride now, because she's tired. That's the way it's been lately. Perhaps it's the spring light and the long walks, but it's more what he said. It wasn't genuine, all that love. It was just something she'd fabricated to make time—no, her life—pass, and afterward she sat there utterly still, and the silence felt like a balm. But now it was time to move on, and the days just kept coming, and she wanted to sit down on the curb and let Kirsten run up staircases eleven and twelve. She won't let herself do that though, but when they reach number fifteen, she starts letting Kirsten say where they come from, contenting herself with standing in the background and helping out if people can't get the coins through the slot. That seems to work okay. The collecting can grows heavier and heavier, and that's great, Kirsten says, even here by Sydvest Station, and then, on the fourth floor of the seventeenth building, they come to an odd door. It's so odd that Kirsten outdoes herself, trying to guess who might live behind it. "Holy shit," says Kirsten, laughing because a rubber skeleton is hanging on the door and the person's called Elsa. Elsa's got a stainless-steel nameplate and a peephole, but the skeleton blocks the hole, so she couldn't see out if she wanted to. Lina tells Kirsten it's the kind of skeleton that'll glow in the dark if all the lights on the stairs go out; her nephew once had an entire can of small insects made from the same sort of rubber. When he'd been tucked in and the light in his room turned off, they glowed everywhere. He'd taped some to the ceiling, while others were under his bed among the Lego bricks, creeping and crawling, illuminated like those fish in the depths of the Mariana Trench. "If it were night, that skeleton would be the only source of light in the entire staircase," Lina says, and Kirsten bursts into laughter and says she's got a notion that Elsa's pretty spry. "She's got a sense of humor," Kirsten says. "She's a party of one," and then she raps on the door, though Lina's about to say that maybe they should skip this door.

But now they've knocked, and at first it's quiet, and there's this listening attitude they've developed, head raised and ear cocked toward the door. It doesn't sound as if anyone's home. Or actually it does. Someone's moving about in the entryway, and just a moment before there were footsteps, and now someone is muttering within. "Someone's muttering in there," Kirsten says, and Lina nods, but just because people mutter in their hallways, that doesn't mean that anyone's coming out, so Kirsten places her mouth close to the glow-in-the-dark rubber and says that they're from the Cancer Society, collecting donations, and "Would you like to support our work?"

There's no answer, but they can tell she's standing right on the other side of the door, Elsa is. "Nothing's happening here," Lina whispers, but Kirsten won't relent and shouts "Hello?" and suddenly there's scratching on the laminate door, a security chain scrapes along its track, the handle's depressed, and then the door opens—and not just a crack. It opens wide, and there she is. Elsa stands erect in her bathrobe on her side of the threshold. It's a small entryway, and she fills the space with her wiry hair and gaping mouth. "Cancer Society," Kirsten says, rattling the can, and Lina wishes she would leave off, for anyone could tell just by looking that Elsa doesn't have a clue what it is they want. She stands there, heavy and bony and with wet strands of hair plastered to her skull, and Lina can see that the only teeth she's got left in her head are the front lower two, and they're the wrong teeth to have left, Lina thinks, unable to keep her eyes off them. "Do you have any spare change?" ventures Kirsten, but Elsa doesn't react as she ought to. She just releases the door handle and goggles at them, and it's unbearable to watch, Lina thinks. It's embarrassing, and now Elsa's starting to rock back and forth in the doorway, perhaps because she's begun to recognize something about the scene, but now it's too late. It's too late because Kirsten's become uncertain and doesn't know how to respond. Kirsten is used to always knowing how to handle a situation, but not with Elsa, and then Kirsten's smile evaporates and Lina can see the sticky floor, and Elsa mutters, but what she says makes no sense, and then Kirsten wants to leave, just leave, and Elsa, who accidentally opened the door for the Cancer Society, loses her grip on her bathrobe. The robe slips to the side so they can see Elsa as she is, and Kirsten wants to leave. She tugs Lina's elbow to signal that they should leave. But they can't just leave, thinks Lina, and she takes a step forward and says, "You must really excuse us for disturbing you. Enjoy the rest of your Sunday," and then she reaches in and closes the door in Elsa's face.

Down on the street there's sunlight, and Lina places herself in the middle of it, while Kirsten remains over by the front door of the building. She says that that was utterly awful. What they'd just gone through is almost too much for her to process, so she says it again: "I've never seen the like. It was awful, wasn't it, Lina?" Lina rummages for the map and doesn't answer, but Kirsten says that no one should be like that, the way Elsa was on the fourth floor. "It's really a disgrace," she says, looking over at the front entrance. "Do you think she has home care?" she asks, but Lina doesn't answer. They're somewhere by Sydvest Station, far from home, and she has the map out and starts walking. There are only two buildings to go, and Kirsten mustn't see that her face is averted, that she feels heat moving deep into her skull and down to her softer parts; that she's thinking about him. She's thinking about him and what he said—that it wasn't love. It couldn't be, he'd said, and here she'd gone and felt precisely as if it were.

BETWEEN
OFFICES

IT WAS IN BOSTON THAT IT HAPPENED THE FIRST TIME. After a shower, I clipped my toenails and stretched out, read a little. When I turned off the light, it began to come over me. I lay on my back, arms a bit out to the sides, legs heavy, relaxed. My body felt good, I sank down into the soft mattress, and a short while later the bed was no longer a bed but bare earth. Thin vegetation grew up around and through me. That's what it felt like. It was a chilly day, far from Boston, there was water nearby, and then the bird came. It perched on one of my ribs. Then it started to peck the flesh from my breastbone. It was a quiet act of devotion, and the sky above me was no longer local but some vast firmament, and I disappeared into it.

The next morning, the first thing I noticed was how well rested I felt. The time difference usually bothers me, but I was wide awake under the showerhead, and down in reception. Forty-eight hours in Boston, and I never managed to see anything but well-scrubbed façades and the branch office. Next to the hotel there was a pleasant park I was able to glimpse from the taxi to the airport. It's always these parks and airports. The fat tourists, the suits, and the neck pillows. The private realm can't be maintained for any length of time but spreads bacterially, from security through the lines for coffee to the loose bowels in the restrooms.

I had a window seat on the morning flight to Minneapolis. I'd never been to Minneapolis before, but one branch resembles the next. I sat comfortably in my seat. Far below me, a lake of oceanic proportions, and the rivers ran, as rivers do, like thick arteries across the terrain. Through slitted eyes I regarded my hands on the armrests. The bones of each hand looked like bone beads; the tendons were milky, and the red was what Mom called *pluckmeat*. The plane's narrow porthole opened out onto the clouds and, seen between them, the prairie below, and I dropped off. I was woken by the usual announcement that we'd begun our descent. Far beneath me, a watercourse was doubling on itself like a large intestine.

Upon landing, I drove straight to the branch office, where I presented targets and lifted the veil on future projects. They'd bought pizza for after. Then we sat there—I with the staff list, they with scarcely concealed discomfort in their faces. "How Nordic," I said, referring to the Scandinavian surnames on the list. "Vestergaard, Dahl, Svensson, Moller," I read aloud, and then they smiled. While these descendants of the Scandinavian exodus gnawed the last soft dough from their pizza crusts, I set their names in historic perspective. "Your name means the western farm, your name's a valley, you're the son of the guy called Sven, and someplace in your relatives' distant past, a man walks around as a miller. My own name is a town by the German border, and I grew up in farm country. When we were going to have a chicken for dinner, my father chopped its head off, and afterward my mother put the entire chicken in a great big pot of boiling water. Then my mother plucked the feathers." I demonstrated with my hands how she did it. "Feathers everywhere, especially the steaming down on her fingers. She couldn't get the down off her fingers, it was a chore," I explained. They were watching me closely, and I imagined some ruddy-faced peasant from a village south of Sæby staring back at me through their emigrant eyes as if I were the parish clerk.

Later, when I was checking in, I noticed the big river I'd seen from the air. It flowed along the foot of a slope here, north of the hotel. "Oh, there's the river," I said to the desk clerk, because I like a friendly atmosphere between me and a hotel. She looked at me suspiciously and said, "Yeah, the Mississippi," and I said, "Really? The Mississippi?" And she said, "Yes sir, the Mississippi." And I said that that came as a surprise, that I hadn't had a clue. In my mind, the great mythic river ran through a sweaty Southern lowland. "This far north?" I asked the clerk, who handed me a key card. "Even the Mississippi has to start somewhere," she said.

I'd wanted to take a rest but busied myself instead with finding a map. It turned out that the clerk was right. It *was* the Mississippi that ran behind the hotel. Its headwaters were in Northern Minnesota. From there it ran for a while almost parallel to the Canadian border and on through Lake Winnibigoshish, whereupon it succumbed to gravity and flowed south, past my hotel window. I usually have a little lie-down after a branch visit, but I was feeling refreshed, so I slid my suitcase in front of the closet, where it would remain standing for the most part unopened, took the elevator down again, and there it was, the Mississippi. Wide and mighty, and with a curiously tidy waterfall a little to the north. I gazed at the foaming water, and then I spotted a bridge with a rust-red railing. It was early dusk, the air was humid, and I could hear cicadas. When I got out to about the middle of the bridge, I positioned myself with my face to the north. Somewhere up there the Mississippi began, and I thought about the round-about path I'd seen the river take on the map. It was as if it couldn't make up its mind at its origin, and then surrendered anyway to the immense downward route.

I've been so many places now that it doesn't matter, I thought. Everything's shifted, but when I was a kid, the best thing I knew was working with poultry. I stuck my hands in among them. Then I might steal the eggs and give them to Mom, until Mom decided to yield to her infections. Dad kept exotic pheasants for a while, and the silver pheasant was hotheaded and easy to tease. When I placed my boot soles up against the fence, it'd come straight over. Its powerful talons against my rubber boot, its beak in a vicious attack. One summer day, when I was walking around barefoot in the grass, I challenged the pheasant. I placed my naked foot against the chicken wire and shouted at it to bring it on. It did. It only wished me ill, but it felt like solicitude, and then I sat down by the wire netting. I gazed into its black eye. I told it that it had barely nipped me. I explained that its attack felt just like being tickled. That it was welcome to try again, it could just attack me, I said. "Attack me," I said again and again, but it just stared back with its black eye, until it seemed to give up. Then it went away.

When I reached the far side, I found a small set of steps down to the Mississippi. The bank consisted of large rocks, and gravel, and tree trunks lay barkless and stranded in the shallows. It smelled of fresh water. My black shoes were glossy in the evening light, and I thought of Mom. Between offices, I try above all not to be touched. I keep disinfectant gel on me, I never dry my hands with cloth towels or air dryers. I bring Kleenex, sneeze into the crook of my arm, rarely stay more than a single night. The Mississippi is no doubt polluted, and the current is strong in a southerly direction. It winds along easily up against the border before gravity takes hold. I would have sunk into it but it would have borne me in the wrong direction, so I just sat there. Later on I lay down. When I'd lain there awhile, the bird came.

THE
FAIRGROUND

THERE'S A STUBBLE FIELD IN FRONT OF THE RENTED house. Over by the side of the small wood is the country fairground, trampled and singed. A fox might make its rounds there, but otherwise it's deserted. Her bare feet are stuffed into the clogs she found in the closet. Both fairground and field have been baking all day in the late-summer sun. It's September now, and when she walks around the field, the stubble scratches her ankles. But now she's standing still, in her trench coat and clogs. The moon's on the rise too.

She thinks a lot about what she did to deserve his silence, which tempted her to assume things that weren't true. And then came the rejection. She'd grown panicky and he'd become cynical, she thinks, gazing across the field to the fairground. They must have had a tombola there, maybe a merry-go-round and roller coaster.

For a time he'd been everything; she supposes it was a kind of obsession. Whatever he did, and even what he thought, haunted her. She read signs in offhand remarks, she researched his past, his possible sorrows. One evening she hid behind the beer taps at a party because his best friend came through the door and looked at her. That face, as horribly unpleasant as foil between one's teeth, was impossible to ignore and she'd hidden behind the kegs. There was a sweet smell of warm grass and public opinion, and it felt as if she were spinning slightly.

Like a suckling pig, she thought. Well spitted, and with an apple jammed in her jaws.

It's September, and she's driven down from the city to the rental. She knows something strange had taken up residence in her. It's something she's known a long time, but the silence gives her no peace. She takes walks along the slopes that drop to the sea, trying to enjoy the sight of cormorants on gillnetting stakes, then heads home to drink tea. The idyllic surroundings provide no relief. On the far side of the stubble field and the wood, the fairground draws her eye. There's a special light over there. The wind raises dust from the field; everyone left the site back in June. The grounds lie there awaiting next year's fair, and such emptiness calls for *some*thing.

I must have been sick, she thinks. The thought occurs to her now and then, even though it was a case of love, just not the love she'd been promised as a child. Back then, she'd imagined that love was just like running through a sprinkler. It tickled, you laughed and felt silly and beautiful at the same time. You were charming and adorable and wove flowers in the wire mesh of the rabbit hutch and won praise for it. No matter what you did, the chosen one would think you were amazing. The happiness was as sweet as peppermint, and it endured. You were extraordinarily dear, and it was the other person's job to make sure everything ended well by not being able to resist the sweetness.

But what she'd been through as an adult belonged to another world entirely. If it wasn't reluctant, then it was dramatic, and in the end the drama became encysted in her. Kept hidden from the world's light, it wreaked havoc, and at some point she convinced herself that it was because he needed love that she had such a great store of it. Yet for him it was merely a flirtation, a matter of discharge, nothing more, she understood that now, and it was actually risky of him. A spark and a merciless drought can set a continent ablaze. He ought to know that. Just take Australia, where civil defense crews wait on tenterhooks in choppers with fat water tanks slung beneath their bellies, anxious and virile, always ready to fly out and stop the craziness from spreading, and now here she stands.

Over on the fairground, the fox prowls at night. It must, for there are always mice in the grass. In the patch where the beer tent stood in June, the ground is pounded down, and when she walks over, she can still catch a whiff of stale beer, and then she sees the rental on the far side of the stubble field. There it squats, reduced to its essence of walls and whitewash. That's the place I'm renting, she thinks. From there I can see everything plainly, yet the house says nothing to her, and then she walks back to it and gazes out toward the fairground. There the mood feels familiar. Maybe it's the empty lot's defenselessness, she doesn't know, but late one night at a party she'd pressed him into a corner. She'd said that they could always be friends. "Friends?" he'd said. "So you want us to be friends?" He didn't say anything else before going out into the hallway and putting on his winter coat, it was snowing, she could see that when he opened the door. Afterward, she thought that he could just as well have said, "Burn in hell," and then she was slowly revolving, trussed up with hooks, while down at her feet a little motor kindly saw to her rotation. Beneath her, the lawn and the beer tent atmosphere. The kids frolicking on the fairground, coltish and clueless, and behind them the wood with its dark chill.

We put flowers in the wire mesh around the rabbits we exhibited behind the fairground, she recalls. We decorated our doll carriages with sweet william, roses, whatever else we could swipe from our mothers' flower beds. Then we paraded through the village and out to the fairground. What were we, six seven eight in our prettiest dresses, and the grownups applauded, some of them on the point of tears. A woman and love, she thinks, and it feels honeyed on the tongue, and she stands at the edge of the stubble and spits. She looks across to the fairground, spitting. The fairground interests her more than the walks above the shore, the cormorants, the beech forest, and it's dawned on her that while it lasted, she was really two people at the same time. One who was as if possessed by love, and one who walked alongside, silent and observing, and sometimes the two would have arguments that the observer always lost, because love bears all things, endures all things, but if I have not love, the lover screamed, I am clanging brass, a sounding cymbal, and the observer made a mental note that horror vacui might be what gets the country's church bells to ring.

A stray ice cream wrapper, over there on the lot, and now a ringdove worming its way through the grass. Empty, she thinks, and I who am so full of things. My doll carriage was pigeon blue, and I decorated it with daisies. We started at the school, and then we marched in procession to the fairground. It smelled of barbecue and dry grass. The parents and teachers ran after us with their cameras, while the boys from school stayed away. I wonder where they were, the boys, as we walked there, a model of compliance. Were they playing soccer, or throwing abandoned bikes into the creek?

She cocks an ear to the evening sky, listening. No boys in the bushes. No boys on the fairground, they're gone, and she tries to make herself taller in order to see it more clearly. The fox is not there, and it's good that the ringdove flies off, for now she is standing on the brink. It's September. In the yard hang apples and black elderberries. Someone's placed a good chair under the chestnut, she could just sit down, but she'd rather stand here with the gas can. It's so quiet, now that everyone's gone home.

COMPACTION
BIRDS

EARLY SATURDAY MORNING I DROVE UP THE COAST from the border, toward Thy. I drove past meadows with flocks of game birds. The geese don't want to migrate anymore. They think it's just as easy to stay in the farmers' fields, so now they hunker there through the winter by the thousand, feeding on winter wheat and old corncobs. They trample, they compact the soil and make it hard.

As I stood on the ferry, crossing the Thyborøn Channel, I was thinking that it was a long way to drive for a woman I'd only spent a single night with. But Anja had been nice when she was waiting on us during the seminar in the national park. She'd wanted to join the dancing after dinner and seemed eager as we walked through the crowberry. She didn't want to do it in the hotel, but there'd been primitive shelters in the area. My performance hadn't been that impressive, yet now her ex-husband had the kids for the weekend. And she had the family summer cottage.

"Come," she'd whispered on the phone.

There's a powerful riptide in the Limfjord. I had to grip the railing tightly on the trip across. The fjord looked as though it were a river flowing toward the North Sea, and up on the Agger Isthmus I saw how everything that no longer had to fly away lay pooling in the lakes, and if she hadn't been standing in the lyme grass by the driveway to a cottage a little farther north, I might well have stayed.

"But here I am," I said as I stepped into the dunes to greet her.

She wore a light-colored dress with small sun-yellow flowers. It was a pretty dress, and she said I looked just like she remembered, and that she was awfully sorry. There'd been some sort of double booking. She'd forgotten that her mother was coming, among others. "I'm awfully sorry," she said, and said it was too bad I'd had my cell phone switched off.

Within the cottage stood a woman in blue, with brushed bangs. She was standing with one of those cast-off mugs you find in summer cottages. It was the mother. In front of her, Anja's sister was gesturing, and behind her sister, a niece sat in a creaking wicker chair. Out on the dunes, her brother-in-law and nephew were kicking a ball.

"The party slipped my mind. My aunt's turning eighty," Anja said, rubbing her forehead. There was a luncheon at a nearby inn. She had to go, she explained. For a couple of hours at least. I could stay and enjoy the cottage. "You're very welcome to join us," Anja's mother said, and stepped closer. "In our family, there's always room for one more at the table."

I shook her mother's hand, then I shook her sister's. I said hi to the niece, and to the brother-in-law when he came in the door with the boy. "Anja says you work at the Society for Nature Conservation," he said. "What are you doing about the barnacle geese?"

I never managed to answer, because Anja pulled me out onto the porch. She said she understood if I'd rather go home now. She was sorry she'd mixed things up so badly, but she was tied down. I said that she looked pretty with those freckles on her nose. She said her aunt had been recently widowed. Then she poked a forefinger into my palm, and I clutched at it.

There was some lighthearted confusion a little while later when Anja kissed me back by the outdoor shower. It wasn't a good kiss. The yellow flowers on the sleeves of her dress seemed to be elsewhere beneath my hands. "I'm so embarrassed," she whispered, and behind the clapboard wall the others were talking about driving to the inn together. There wasn't enough room in her brother-in-law's Audi, so I ended up in the passenger seat of Anja's car, her mother behind me with her hands on my headrest.

We took the main coast road north, trailing her brother-in-law. We drove like this for a while through the national park. From the backseat, Anja's mother spoke of the view and the place names, and she wanted to know exactly where I lived. "Tøndermarsken," I said. "By yourself, right?" she asked, and I confirmed that I was a widower. I also mentioned that my wife had been a pastor, but that seemed to land awkwardly. Then Anja's mother gave a recapitulation of some article she'd read in the weekly paper. It had to do with wolves and how they communicate across long distances by howling. "They're social creatures," she said.

In this way we drove along behind the brother-in-law until he turned into a rest stop. Anja conferred with him, while her mother worried about not getting there in time for the first course. As for me, I was looking at the flowers on Anja's dress and the clusters of game birds lifting off from the vegetation. In the winter they would stick around: compaction birds.

What had happened was that the brother-in-law had gone north by mistake, and after a half-hour excursion in the wrong direction, we arrived at the inn well into the first course. There was a burst of applause and general merriment when we crossed the floor. If I'd known who the other guests were, I would have attempted a bit of clowning, but Anja's was the only face present that was somewhat familiar, and she wasn't looking up.

Seats had been set aside for the family. I sat down in the only available chair at a table that wasn't the head table. To my left was a little man who introduced himself as a cousin from the other side of the family. He explained that it was his wife's place I'd taken. "She never goes anywhere anymore," he said, and then I turned to my right, where a bearded man was seated. After that, a fish landed on my plate. "Cheers!" exclaimed a wrinkled face across from me. It belonged to a woman. "It's a good thing you made it."

I patted Anja's hand every time it rested on my shoulder in passing. "I'm terribly sorry about this," she whispered, and at such moments there were eyes upon us, so Anja stopped doing it, and I didn't feel I could go over to her.

In this fashion, the luncheon proceeded. Now and then I went to the restroom to make the time pass, and it was when I was trying to urinate again that a man stepped into the stall next to mine and unzipped. A profuse pissing commenced. I finished up discreetly, flushed, and opened the stall door, but not fast enough to escape the brother-in-law.

"Oh, it's you!" he said, coming over to the sink. "Now we've pissed together." I said it was almost as good as being blood brothers, after which we returned to the party, where the coffee had been served.

"What are you people planning to do about those barnacle geese?" he asked, pulling me down at the deserted end of a table. "And the whooper swans and the pinkfeet? I've had to resow my fields. My neighbor too." I glanced around for Anja, who was being detained at the head table. "What do the ag associations suggest?" I asked. "Can you spray for them?" he said, and laughed.

I have this conversation every day, and I pointed out that it was really due to climate change. Then he wanted to know if it was also the climate's fault that the wolves had come north to harass his cows. I explained, as I usually do, that wolves have adapted to a Europe at peace, and he maintained, as no doubt he usually does, that he didn't want to let his kids play in the tree plantation anymore. Finally he said, "I hope you have a great view from your ivory tower, but you should know that we're rather fond of Anja. Why don't you try a widows' ball down in Southern Jutland instead?"

Out of the corner of my eye I could see Anja. The yellow flowers spread across the dress fabric and resembled creeping potentilla. That was something she had loved, and I always see it when I go out into the marsh. It blossoms abundantly in the groundcover, and there was something about her face, especially her mouth. Yet restless, that she was. Couldn't be in the place she found herself. Once when we were at a dinner, she whispered to me that she felt naked without her vestments and wanted to go home. She had a way of leaving me, also in bed. When her legs began to get twitchy under the comforter, I'd place a hand on one of them and say, "A little while yet," but it was no use, and now here was this woman Anja, sitting in the bosom of her family, tearing a napkin to pieces.

I suggested that we take a little walk, down to the water. She cast a sidelong glance at her aunt and mother and ended up standing on the beach, backlit at the water's edge. As she stood there in silhouette, we agreed that it would be best if she drove me back to the cottage. My car was there, after all. "I feel terribly embarrassed," she said a couple of times on the way, and I said she shouldn't. "I did get a nice drive out of it."

It was still warm when I drove south, and somewhere on the Agger Isthmus I pulled over at a scenic rest stop. A light breeze was flowing across the terrain. Into the landscape went a path, and I followed it until it vanished in the dunes. Then I took off my shoes. Down by the breakers, flocks of gulls. When they weren't climbing the wind they stood frozen on the beach, gazing outward. Oddly abandoned and always on the lookout for a fish. After a while I pissed and went back to the car. There I sat, next to Route 181 southbound. The key in the ignition, the sunset, the night.

PERSHING SQUARE

THIS HEAT, NO PEACE. SEEN FROM THE HOTEL ROOM window, the palm trees tilt. Down in Pershing Square is a tower that someone's erected, with a bright Christmas ornament at the top. At first she thought it was a bell tower, but the ornament can't ring. The first evening, when the heat eased off, she walked guardedly down Grand Avenue. When she came to a cross street, someone yelled, "Hey girl, are you European?" and then she turned and went back to the hotel. She's no girl any more, that's obvious. But she *is* European, though how would he know? It might be her pale skin, but then she could just as easily be Canadian. Which wouldn't be the worst thing in the world.

On the streets of downtown LA she sees all sorts. What they have in common are their faces, their gaits, and the shape of their limbs. But more than anything they share indifference. The insane and the addicted fill the avenues. If she should collapse, no one would notice. A middle-aged white woman, hands outstretched and pleading faintly, would be just another wretch downtown. The sun is blazing and she moves around slowly, a bit stiffly, sweating. I'm moving as if I'm one of them, she thinks, and then she returns to the hotel and lays herself down on the bed.

There was a time when the heat wasn't so hard on her, but now it's combined with a new condition in her body. It's her heart, it's got a flutter, or something in there is pressing, and on one of her first evenings she met up with a colleague. They had a beer together at a sidewalk restaurant. The idea had been to talk about some new program development in connection with the conference. The whole time he was checking his messages. There she sat, pretending to watch the street life until a friend of his showed up. Then they chatted a little, but there was a moment, while the friend had his back turned, fiddling with his phone, and her colleague was gazing down at his, when she felt so minimally present that she leaned across the table and asked where the bathroom was. Her colleague looked up and smiled, confused.

Afterward, at the hotel, she determined that her heart was beating heavily, and that she was tired of straight men. Years ago, a psychologist she'd gone to had told her that, when she met a man, she should avoid being so clever. She hadn't understood this advice. Then the psychologist, who was a hetero male, explained that because men were afraid of rejection—and because their penises meant so much to them—they were anxious that a smart woman might laugh at them because they masturbated out in the bathroom. That's the phrase he used, "out in the bathroom." "Men think," the psychologist said, "that less intelligent women won't mind their sexual behavior so much."

He had his legs crossed, she recalled, and she could also recall saying that that couldn't be true. "That's just the way it is," the psychologist said, and the entire drive home she thought about an episode of *Dr. Phil* she'd once seen. It featured a woman not unlike herself. She sat on stage and lamented the fact that men rejected her because she was intelligent. Dr.

Phil affirmed this without hesitation. Then the woman said it was wrong and unfair. Then Dr. Phil asked, "But do you want to be right, or do you want to be happy?" Whereupon the audience applauded wildly.

She often imagined men jerking off in some nearby bathroom. Sometimes she would get an urge to tell them that, her intellect notwithstanding, it didn't bother her that they masturbated. Yet she was tired of the haggle for respect, so when it was only her third day in LA, she skipped the conference sessions and called Pete and Anthony. They became giddy, as only they could. The palm trees swayed, and now she's at the hotel, looking down on Pershing Square. They'd built a tower there and placed a Christmas ornament up at the top. It's a curious tower, pointless, she thinks, and that morning, before the restlessness returned, she walked slowly around downtown. "Hey lady, be safe!" shouted one of the ill, and she really isn't—safe that is. But perhaps if she'd been Canadian. It's safer in Canada than most places. Maybe it's the vast landscapes, the distances. Maybe it's the gun laws, Newfoundland, and the figure skaters. She was born in Vojens, and her mother was treasurer of the hockey club. She was also responsible for the Christmas raffle. Sometimes hockey-playing boys from other countries would stay with them. Once between Christmas and New Year's they hosted two brothers from Toronto. They could only speak English, but back then she didn't dare to. She can remember the combination of the Christmas tree and their longish dark hair in the large living room. And she can remember that the one brother had to borrow some socks in order to sleep. These days she thinks of him often, when she herself is going to sleep. She has a pair of socks on right now. It's ninety-five degrees outside, but operating the air conditioner is a challenge: "Hey girl, are you European?"

"No, Canadian," she'll say if they should ask her again the next time she ventures out. And it's not unlikely. After less than a week downtown, she can already distinguish one homeless person from the next. She recognizes them by their walks, their haunts, the particular ways they protect themselves from the world: the big woolen hats, the winter jackets, the out-of-place carry-on luggage, and beneath the Christmas ornament in Pershing Square she saw a woman with a top hat and floral umbrella direct an invisible drum corps with such battered grace, she had half a mind to follow. Perhaps if she'd been younger, and Anthony and Pete had been there, she thinks, slowly sitting up in bed. They came and got her the other evening. Threw their arms around her and demanded a guided tour of the hotel. When she confided that she felt heavy, Pete squeezed her shoulder, while Anthony laughed— "Come on girl, you're in LA"—and then they went out into the stifling heat together.

They'd chosen a restaurant on Broadway, where the bread was shaped like sea turtles and the food had to be retrieved from a labyrinth. It was good food, and plentiful, but it was impossible to deal with all that entertainment. She also had a hard time looking down at her plate. A black cavity opened up beneath her when she tried. Like a hole in the ice, she thought, and looked up at the ceiling, but that didn't help. As they ate, Pete and Anthony narrated scenes from their life together. In some of them, she appeared as a walk-on from the old days, and then she would try to laugh along with them, but at some point she got to her feet. "I'm just going to stand up and talk," she said. "My legs are starting to fall asleep," she said, though that wasn't true. It was the hole in the ice, she was scared of sliding down into it. Anthony had teased her a bit. She looked funny, he said, and she considered asking whether they knew a good doctor, but she couldn't deal with the consequences of seeing a doctor, so she just stood.

It was while she was standing there that she caught sight of a man down on another level of the restaurant. He was a relatively old man. Brown and wrinkled from the sun, and he had hair that was much too black, cut in that style that men had when she was a girl. Glam rock hair, and he stood chatting with women who had been variously patched together. None of them were pretty. Everyone she'd met downtown looked as if they were a bit ill, and the fellow down there on the other level was as thin as a razorblade.

It got to be too much for her, so she'd asked Anthony and Pete to take her back to the hotel. They had done so, though she can't remember what they talked about as they walked. She was thinking mostly about how, back when they were young, Pete and Anthony gave her lessons in men. This is how they liked to be stroked, this is how they thought about certain situations. She recalled that their basic principle for relations with men, regardless of sexual orientation, was that they had fragile egos. Decent men *knew* they had fragile egos, so when someone trod on their toes, they'd take a step back before reacting. In that way, decent men kept themselves under surveillance for any misplaced aggression. But bad men were men who reacted immediately whenever they felt insecure or something offended their vanity. They were men who felt they had the right to lash out at anyone and anything. Some of them verbally, others physically. No matter what, just stay away from category number two, they explained to her. A man only has his pride, they said, and at the time she thought that sounded nice. If her body hadn't felt so heavy on the walk back to the hotel, she would have asked about it again, but it was all she could manage to tuck her arm under Pete's and declare herself tired. So that was that, and now she's lying here and longing for Canada. In California, and maybe all of the US, people think of Canada as somewhere nondramatic. Hollywood movies often have jokes about Canada. The jokes concern Canadians' unflappability. Their policemen wear red coats and ride horses. The English speakers have a distinctive way of saying their *o*'s. You can especially hear it in the word *sorrow*. SORE-*oh*, they say, as if the word itself wanted to wrap its arms around you. More than anything else, the two Canadian hockey brothers had been well mannered. They were good-looking, with that longish dark hair, and they carried their plates out to the kitchen sink. They thanked her mother for their dinner and made their own beds. Boring kids, she thinks, seen from today's vantage, and she stretches her legs underneath the sheets so that her socks poke out the bottom. The one boy had stood in the doorway to her room the evening he asked about the socks. And she understood what he was asking for and got a pair of woolen ones from her mother's room. "Thank you," he said when she gave them to him. "We get cold feet in Canada," he said, and then she nodded, he smiled, they went into their respective rooms and slept, and now she's lying here looking at the tower with the Christmas ornament. That ornament can't ring, and the lights go on in the square below. A woman is walking around down there with top hat and umbrella, and a thin black figure passes through it all like a straight razor. She places a hand on her chest, something's pressing inside, and there is ice on the lakes in Canada.

HONEYSUCKLE

THE YEAR BEFORE HE MET HER, HE'D BEEN DOING research on the immune system at NYU, as part of his medical studies. It had become a habit for him to make his way home through a Hasidic neighborhood in Brooklyn. They didn't welcome strangers, but he was discreet and would act as if he were on some errand. The women went about in long dresses, and now and then he found an opportunity to observe a couple of them on a street corner. Drably dressed, no makeup, long skirts and sleeves. To most Western men they might seem lacking in imagination, but there he stood, watching them with a palpable erection.

He had that way of coming to a standstill over there. In July, when the heat was at its height, he sometimes came to a halt by the big flower beds in Central Park. The irises stretching upward, the scent of roses, and in one place honeysuckle. He would stand there in the sun, thinking of his parents' yard in Risskov. Perhaps he was longing for home, but mostly it was for the way everything seemed when seen from the street. Or when one looked at the family in old photos. These days his mother tried to avoid the camera, and his father didn't own one. He devoted himself to gardening instead. In front of the house was an area with pruned yews and cedars, while roses were tended in the backyard. On the south gable end a honeysuckle grew. When it was in flower, its sweet odor settled over the yard, and then he didn't know how to feel about anything.

But when he returned to Aarhus in '88, he discovered her on a couch in Hasle. She had a withdrawn face. It didn't really occur to him till afterward, but she did. The thick lenses, the black hair, the smallness of her eyes. She was sitting with two girlfriends on a couch. The other two were good-looking, he remembers, yet next to the black-haired one they quickly faded away. Tea was passed round, and cookies, and she sat by the padded armrest in a summer dress and said she was studying to be a social worker. He would be continuing his research in immunology at the university hospital, and he couldn't stop staring at her. It was the way her mouth moved, the words disconnected from her eyes. Out in the hallway, he asked her how much she could actually see, and then she placed a fist in front of both eyes. She did it to illustrate that there was a small tunnel of clear vision, there where her fingers didn't close completely. She'd been born that way, she explained; her eyes weren't properly alive, and it was true. There was something untouched about her, and on the bike ride home it struck him that her face was withdrawn, and that that was why he almost couldn't sit to pedal.

In the days that followed it was hard to find any peace. Her reserved face haunted him. He masturbated in the bathroom, in bed, in the greenhouse in his parents' yard during Sunday dinner, while the other family members sat intoxicated with the scent of honeysuckle. They were sitting on the patio, his brother and his brother's family, Uncle Tyge with his new wife, his mother and father at either end of the table. When he had finished, he came to a standstill. He didn't feel like leaving the greenhouse. From inside, through the grapevines and ripe tomatoes, the scene looked like a summer dinner in some carefully tended family. The large salad bowl, the leaves gleaming with oil, the white wine, and just behind it his mother with her face. Because the family had these blood vessels that lay on the surface of their cheeks, his mother's condition could be discerned from the greenhouse. The edema, and the contrast with his father and all his talk about the hedge trimmer.

Before he left, he got them to stand in the sun with their backs against the south gable. "We never take family photos anymore," he said. At first his mother didn't want to be in it. He should at least take it from over by the sundial, she said. So he did that, took up a position there, and then he zoomed in on her and clicked. There she stood, blossoming in the sweet smell.

But the girl from Hasle was called Annette, and she wasn't like that. She couldn't see much, though that didn't matter because he could see for them both, and on the whole it suited him just fine that he was allowed to be a man who was invisible, yet present. The sort of man who would always be there with a light hand on the small of his woman's back. Nor did it matter that he was a mere mist on her half-dead retinas. That way he wouldn't be judged for his grimaces when he lost control. It was a heartening thought, and it made him cross his legs on the number 8, in the seat reserved for those with restricted mobility, where once a heavily made-up girl had got him to stand up by claiming she was a semiotician and had tired legs. That was before America, before the faraway but well-planned walks, and that kind of girl didn't interest him anymore.

Annette was studying to be a social worker with help from the Institute for the Blind. She came from Randers. Her hair was black, her face white, and her body present in a slightly provincial way, and he couldn't ask her to the movies. Instead he took her to concerts in Tangkrogen. A blanket on the grass, white wine, and his hand, which he often rested on hers. As they sat there, she would sing along now and then, or listen as he talked of his family in Risskov. His father was a doctor, he said, and his mother taught in a kindergarten. In his free time his father was an avid gardener, an identity he could imagine himself taking on, he admitted. In any case, he had gone on some lovely walks in Central Park when he was studying immunology in the US. The lilies there were gorgeous, the scent of lavender almost Provençal. Annette loved the smell of flowers too, she said, and while she described the size of the sunflower she'd once grown in Randers, he pictured the Hasidic women. They'd stood on that street corner in their black skirts, far from Aarhus. Not shaved bald yet, not wearing wigs and headscarves. Still with their dark hair tied back. High-neck blouses, long sleeves, ballerina flats. As they stood there, they swished their skirts back and forth, glancing uncertainly about for fathers and brothers, smiling faintly in their modesty. He'd had a similar experience once before, when he'd found himself standing in line behind a veiled woman in the supermarket on Guldsmedgade. He hadn't wanted her to leave the store, though usually he wasn't attracted to that type. The faces of most young women with veils seemed to him ambiguous, though on the other hand he'd recorded a documentary about the Amish on VHS. He'd watched that documentary often after he came back from the US (*their bonnets, their bonnets, those braids, their bonnets*), but he couldn't tell Annette that. Nor could he tell her about the photo of his mother under the honeysuckle. How he'd had it blown up and stuck it up on the fridge in his apartment, the glowing pores, the white wine sheen. When he gazed at the picture, he could recall how she smelled when she kissed him goodnight.

The first time they did it, him and Annette, was in her room next to the kitchen in Hasle. Nobody else was home, but she wanted the lights off, so it was lucky it was summer. He was able to push her far enough to the left on the pillow that the light from the window struck her. There she lay like a pale blotch in the midsummer night, and he removed her glasses. The stripped, absent face excited him, and while her gaze fluttered about trying to locate him, she told him she'd never done this before. Then he stroked her hair, until a faint expression of gratitude appeared on the face below. A small picture of the effect of his caress, and it made his erection so hard, he was forced to raise himself on one elbow. Then his hand down in her panties. Then the fuck. And he fucked her till her mouth became a gaping O and her black hair crackled with static against the striped bedsheet.

No, she didn't really have a face until he engaged her, and she didn't really have a face afterward. Yet somewhere in between there was a sweet blossoming, an identity squeezing its way out, a wet mouth, tears, passionate pain. He granted her a will, trained on him, and later he biked home through Aarhus, satisfied that he would keep her. And thus the years passed. He'd kept her, and God he had fucked her often. Sometimes when he was sitting under the honeysuckle in their yard in Risskov, watching her stare blindly at the robot mower, her face a bit flushed and swollen with fluid, yet still quite anonymous, it would hit him just how many times he'd fucked her. It was incredible that her face still seemed to exist only with his help. Her speech had improved, no doubt about that. Her attempts to act independently in the world, and the sudden fits of weeping that could drive her from the table, were both signs of individual character. But the rest of it, he thought, was a continuum.

ON NARROW PAVED PATHS

THE FIRST OF JUNE, EINAR WAS DIAGNOSED WITH cancer. The second of June, Alice rang up their circle of friends and told them that Einar had been diagnosed with cancer, and to judge by his emaciated state he had nothing to bring to the fight, so it must be terminal. In any case it would be best if Einar, who had no wife or children, was admitted to a hospice as quickly as possible, that was Alice's opinion. Her own husband had died in the hospice, "And those were his best days," she said on the phone when her listeners had sat down heavily, on the sofa or in a kitchen chair, with a "Poor Einar."

On the fifth of June, Alice walked along the neighborhood's narrow paved paths to Einar's, where the door was never locked. She went through the yard and into the kitchen, and here she found the invalid with a schnapps and a cheroot. The invalid appeared anxious and apathetic, and Alice met him with warm thin hands and a steady gaze. Then they smoked together, while Alice told him how to deal with a serious illness. Her father had been a dentist and there was nothing to be done but take things as they came, yet Einar had a faraway look in his eyes. He stared at the birdfeeder outside the window and said, "When Mother died, a robin appeared at the feeder. It kept coming back that entire winter. It was Mother who was visiting me." That same evening, Alice rang around and said she feared that Einar's cancer had metastasized to the brain.

The tenth of June, Einar went to a doctor's appointment with his sister to discuss treatment options. It was in the morning, and what the doctor said was that as long as he drank schnapps, they couldn't treat him. In the evening Alice called everyone and said that the sister had found empty schnapps bottles and flattened boxes of wine in the invalid's home, but not much in the way of food. "You can't be cured if you don't eat," Alice explained, that's what her father had always said. That's also what she'd always said herself, back when her son was little. "You've got to have something to bring to the fight."

The next day, Alice went along the neighborhood's narrow paths to the invalid, who sat askew in a chair in the kitchen and talked about all the years he was looking forward to. The future unfolded itself for Einar, and he spoke of it in hazy images. On the table were some tranquilizers the doctor had prescribed. He fingered them and expounded on what was to be planted in the kitchen garden next year. He also spoke about how he was now going to be cured. A woman he went to croquet with on Tuesdays had dropped by with a guide to eating yourself free from cancer. Lemons and baking soda in particular were known to work miracles. The woman had also brought provisions. Alice could have a look herself, and she did: Einar's refrigerator was full of lemons and baking soda, but Alice easily swept the contents into a garbage bag. Afterward she sat beside him and laid a thin hand over his. "My father was a dentist," she said, "and the only thing baking soda can save is a cake." Later, Alice went home and called up the woman with the lemons. She asked her straight out to pack it in, though she needn't have sounded so harsh. That's what she thought afterward, before she called the others. After all, the invalid had chosen the schnapps over the lemons, and the prescribed tranquilizers lay on the table like mints. To judge by Einar's condition, he wasn't able to figure out his doses. "We just have to hope he manages to get into a hospice," Alice told everyone who was following Einar's last days, and then she went to bed and slept like a rock.

Every day from the twelfth to the nineteenth, Alice went over to see Einar. He was lying in his bed more often now, which made his feet easier to get at. She removed his socks and massaged his feet, lumpy as they were, because it felt so nice, she knew it did. As she sat there at the foot of Einar's bed and talked about her father, who'd been a dentist, about her devoted years as a schoolteacher, about her deceased husband, and about her son, who'd been sweet as a child, her fingers were busy pinching and patting. The big tom that always hung about Einar was easy enough to shoo off the bed. Then it stalked around beneath the bed and glowered at Alice, while up on the bed she spoke of the future. "I for instance have my funeral completely sorted," Alice told Einar, who floated in and out of a schnapps fog. "I know precisely which songs they'll sing," and Einar opened an eye with difficulty and said, "But I still have long to live."

That's what he said on the nineteenth of June, but the next day he had an appointment at the hospital. Alice only received a summary, because it was his sister who accompanied him to the doctor. And the doctor said there was nothing they could do, that Einar should go home and make the most of his remaining time. Those were his words, according to the sister's summary, and in the evening Alice called around the circle and said, "Now we have to hope he manages to get a hospice place." Afterward, when she'd hung up the phone, she sat for a while staring out into the midsummer darkness, and without realizing it she hummed, "I get so happy when the sun is shining."

A few days later, Einar stopped drinking schnapps. He had no more thirst for schnapps but he wanted his cheroot, and the anti-anxiety drugs. So he sat, with cheroot and water glass, skin and bone, in his kitchen, looking from the dear cat to the feeder outside the window while his sister tended to his daily needs. Alice appeared at regular intervals in the front doorway, dressed in a black turtleneck sweater, menthols in her purse. Her hair was neatly gathered at her nape, her feet large, a bit like a crow's, thought Einar, when the Midsummer's Eve bonfires left only Alice to help him use the bathroom. He had to pee all the time, and here's what she said the next morning: "Everything runs right through Einar."

On the twenty-eighth of June, Einar had a birthday party, propped up in an armchair with some outdoor cushions. He received presents and wishes for the future, he received a piece of layer cake, and from a distant acquaintance whom Alice had called up, he received a preprinted card with the word CON-GRATULATIONS on the front in gold glitter. *I understand that you've been struggling with your health,* the acquaintance had written on the card, *but I'm sure it'll all turn out fine. Doctors nowadays are so clever.* Einar read the card and tucked it under the glass of water that later would run right through him.

In the days that followed, Einar slept lightly most of the time, to the sound of rain on the roof. When Alice stood unannounced one morning in the hall, the sister told her that now they needed quiet, no more visitors. Everyone on the phone list picked up, and Alice said, "We've started sending unannounced visitors away, no more callers!" Not counting the woman with the lemons, everyone said it was good that Einar had Alice. Alice did not dispute this. She hoped to have someone like herself with her when, someday, she was dying, even though she would prefer to enter a hospice. It was so pleasant to be in a hospice, and that night she dreamt she could fly, lustrous in her black clothes, free, she felt, and eternal. Beneath her the plowed fields, the sand beaches, the freeway verges, all of it now and forever her domain. Yet on the first of July she woke weighted down by a bronchitic cough.

On the fourth day of July, Alice met the sister on one of the neighborhood paths, and the sister said that it wouldn't be long now. She asked Alice to go home and wait, and Alice went home and announced, "It won't be long now."

Late that evening, the family gathered with Einar's comfort and joy, his cat, at his deathbed. Hands were held, a psalm was sung, and at four o'clock in the morning, Einar died in his sleep in the firm belief that he had a future before him.

·   ·   ·

On the seventh of July, Alice had a great deal to see to. She needed information about the funeral, she needed to order a wreath, and she also needed to iron her black gabardine pants. She was in the grocer's several times, where she had to tell the same story again and again, about how the entire thing had ended so peacefully. As for Einar's beloved tomcat, rumor had it that it sat at the dead man's feet, meowing. The rumor caught up with Alice by the revolving door of the supermarket, and the family shouldn't have to worry about that cat. It was past noon when Alice turned up at the dead man's house with a carrier. The sister seemed red-eyed and relieved, and Alice said, "From now on, the cat officially lives with me," and the mortician who poked his head out from the dead man's bedroom also seemed relieved. It wasn't easy getting the cat stuffed into the carrier, it snarled and scratched her. But once she was home she put it in the bathroom and called the vet. He had an open spot late in the afternoon, and the cat got its needle and died in its sleep in the belief that it had a future before it.

On the eleventh of July there was a funeral. It was held at two o'clock in the afternoon, and people came in good time. They drifted into the church to secure themselves seats, as the deceased had been well liked. The nearest relations sat in one of the front pews, and at 1:35 p.m., Alice slipped through the people arriving in the church porch, stepped confidently across the memorial sprays and wreaths, and made her way to the pew closest to the coffin. Then she sat in front of the family with folded hands, looking at the large arrays of lilies with their silk sashes.

·   ·   ·

It was a suitably depressing funeral coffee, with rolls and cold cuts, kringles, a dram for those who required it. There was smoking in the yard, and here Alice explained to the circle what had happened in Einar's last days, and what they should remember to be thankful for: that it went quickly, that he'd been free of pain, that the cat had found a new home. Then each of them departed, ready to face their everyday cares once more, and around eleven on that first evening of Einar's everlasting life, Alice plopped down in front of the window by her kitchen table and felt empty inside. A small wren bobbed in the yew beneath the windowsill, and Alice felt as if she were hungry. But no snacking now, she told herself, and then she took out her notebook, wrote *Einar buried, the cat put down, good one can be of assistance,* and turned out the light.

INSIDE
ST. PAUL'S

SUN AT THE ZENITH ABOVE ST. PAUL'S, AND HE GAZES at a black Madonna, while she bakes in the sunshine out on the square. He'd even read up on the churches, back home. The dome is majestic, and his plan had been for them to experience it from the inside. The black Madonna's nursing her infant, her nipple moist with saliva. It's a video installation, and the lighting in here is soft, like in a forest. You're not allowed to take pictures. That doesn't matter to him. She's the one with the camera on her phone, and she's sitting out there with sunscreen on her face, staring into it.

He wants to go down into the crypt, to Lord Nelson, and it's simple enough to find his way there. The crypt is arranged so that, sooner or later, you end up down by Lord Nelson. He lies in his own chamber: black sarcophagus, high plinth encircled by white columns. He's been granted his very own starry vault and coronet, *Horatio Nelson, 1st Viscount*. You can walk round and round his mighty sepulchre, and that's what people do, most of them with headphones on in the midst of an audio tour. But he has an urge to touch it, and he rests his hand on the tomb.

It surprises him to find the sarcophagus slightly warm; he thought it would be cool. Out on the square the sun is broiling. There she sits, even though it's shady in St. Paul's. Nelson lies inside with his one arm, and he'd imagined a chilly place of preservation. Like a larder. Or at least a temperature like under the bleachers. It's cold there; he knows. As a boy, he always went to the rink with his father and older brother. While they sat up in the bleachers, yelling slogans at the starting forwards, he found his way down beneath them. The players skated in wide, confident circles behind the blue line. They slammed into the boards so hard that the plexiglass shook, and he got a couple of coins from his father for candy during each intermission. Then he could stand in the line by the candy counter and figure out what he'd buy during the next intermission. He really liked the intermissions. The Zamboni would drive around and transform the scuffed rink into a shiny sheet of ice. Once the game started up again, he'd disappear beneath the bleachers. It was extra chilly down there, and he'd expected a similar temperature at Nelson's tomb. Or at least a temperature where you might expect that his cadaver would be well preserved; that he wasn't lying inside cooking. Once on TV he watched a 400-year-old corpse being lifted out of a sarcophagus. It had been subjected to temperature conditions so ideal, the body had simply dried out. Like one of the mice you find under the eaves, intact. The conservator took a knife and opened up the body. Then he began to fish out the corpse's desiccated excrement. It looked like a beach pebble. A large beach pebble, or a hockey puck for that matter. At home his brother would dribble the puck out on the patio. On occasion he was allowed to borrow a stick and try to steal the puck. He struck his brother with the stick once, it might have been by accident. Then his brother threw himself on top of him, pinning him to the paving stones with a knee on each arm. He let the threat of a loogie dangle above him, till he tried to spit back up at his brother and the spit landed in his own face.

Beneath the stands he could see everything that the men and their girlfriends with the blue eye shadow threw down through the gaps between the benches. He studied the objects piece by piece, and if you walked all the way to the left or the right, you came to one of the places where the ice stuck out under the boards, at the round corners of the rink. On the small triangles there he could slide and skate in his sneakers without getting in anyone's way. A little triangle of ice up against the boards and *swoosh* he glided forward, *swoosh* he glided back, while they thundered against the plexiglass: lumpy gloves and visors, jockstraps and shoulder pads, spitting, sweating, and *swoosh* he'd disappear beneath the bleachers.

It feels curious to picture himself standing so close to Lord Nelson. That he's lying in there, one-armed and one-eyed. He read up on the Battle of Copenhagen at home. He knows that Nelson sailed south of the Middle Ground shoal on Maundy Thursday in 1801, and that the ships of the British fleet had marvelous names: *Elephant, Defiance, Ganges* and *Monarch, Agamemnon* and *Désiree*. He built models of Nelson's ships as a boy. In the kits, the cannons were so small he had to use tweezers. Once he lost one of the tiny cannons in a glass of fruit drink and got the notion to swallow it. So that's what he did. It was such a tiny cannon that he never felt it in his throat, and if it didn't lodge in his tissue, he must have passed it in the bathroom. He didn't tell her, out on the square, the bit about the fruit drink, though he did rattle off the names of Nelson's ships. She wasn't interested. He nudged her a little, asking her if she'd heard about the time Nelson put the telescope to his blind eye. Then she looked at him, and he raised his fist to one eye, adjusting an imaginary spyglass. "I do not see the signal," he said.

He said it to be funny, but then she had to visit the restroom, and he had to watch her phone. She's been playing this game where you pop balloons, and now he's standing here beside Lord Nelson. He's got a finger on the sarcophagus. He's probably nothing but a skeleton with clothes on. A weakling to look at by now, and his brother used to play hockey with a spindly boy. When he came over and stood in their kitchen, he was no more than a brushstroke in the air, but hockey gear can optimize anything. The question is whether you dare to body-check. Beneath the bleachers, it smelled of the damp and the dark and ice on concrete. Lord Nelson would've been better preserved there, yet here he is. Dead, and easily defeatable. In life he was impressive, and the sarcophagus is imposing. It'd be nice if she were standing next to him now. There was a time when they always visited churches together. Ten years ago, she would have been standing at his side. In her bag she'd have juice cartons, disinfected hankies, chapstick. There was a time when she never left home without fruit in her purse. He's given her children, and they've never wanted for anything. The last thing he saw outside was her biting into an almond croissant, washing it down with scalding coffee, and reaching for her phone. Who can drink coffee in this heat? he wonders, closing his eyes for a moment. He sees the rink's little surplus triangles. He watches his sneakers gliding across the ice. He leans up against the boards and here they come, the players, hammering into the plexiglass. They fight with sticks and shoulder pads. He can smell the ammonia, and he's so small that no one can see him. Then he forms a gob of spit behind his teeth. He leans in to the boards, and then he spits. It's a paltry gob and not exactly epic as it slides first down the plexiglass, then the marble. Nope, it's not exactly epic.

THE FREEZER CHEST

WHEN I THINK ABOUT IT, THE FREEZER CHEST, IT'S WITH a sensation of the ferry rocking and the North Sea beneath us, black because it was January, and then the artificial lighting of the lounge where they were sitting, Mark and the others—Starling, Henrietta, Poul, and Susanna—and where I was also sitting, with our English teacher, Bo, who found me interesting to talk to, for, as he said, "One would never know that you were so young." But in any case, they sat together over in a corner and it was 1989, the DJ had left, no one wanted to dance, it was late and a long way to Harwich, and then he went to bed anyway, the English teacher, and I was actually friends with Henrietta, so I wasn't sure what to do, but it was then that he called me over to the group, Mark did, and said he wanted to tell me the story of the freezer chest.

I should have seen it coming, for he made no secret of not liking me. Once he'd said it in the middle of the cafeteria, and he'd said it straight out: "I don't like you." It had been a simple statement, and the place had grown quiet, even though Henrietta was there too, and I thought she'd protest because you couldn't just say things like that, we weren't twelve anymore. This was high school after all and I was eighteen, most of us were, but there were a few older students who had dropped out to see the world, or to learn a trade, and had now taken up their schoolbooks again, and Mark was one of them; I think he was twenty-five. But she didn't say a word, Henrietta, and so I said it myself, that you couldn't just sit there and say that sort of thing, but then Mark looked at me and said you certainly could, *somebody* ought to. He was sitting there with a classmate who was preparing for teachers college, while Henrietta ate her potato salad and got herself a Coke, and the would-be teacher never said boo.

But then Mark was coming along on the study trip to London, and I knew that it would prove difficult, because not only did Mark not like me, but all the others liked him a lot, and even though I was friends with Henrietta I'd have to hang out with the English teacher, who claimed that he'd once flown with the Royal Canadian Air Force, and as he was telling me how he'd ended up there and how age-related farsightedness had come between him and reenlistment, I looked over at the little group gathered around Mark. Henrietta was there too, laughing every time he said something, but then when the English teacher had gone to his bunk, he called me over, Mark did, and told me the story of the freezer chest.

It began with him explaining how he'd once been a talented guitarist with a promising career stretching out before him. He was in demand among solo performers, and the reason he was the oldest person in our school was that he'd had a life beforehand, on the road with his guitar. It had been an exciting but hard life, with all the late nights at small clubs, he said. Did I believe him? I shrugged my shoulders. He was difficult to fathom sometimes and you never knew what would come next with him, that much I had learned, because once Henrietta and I had gone to visit him up in his flat. Henrietta had been wanting to visit Mark privately—she'd talked about it a lot, just as she talked a lot about incest, since it was around that time that it first became okay to talk about it, the fact that it existed. Henrietta had seen something about it on TV, she said, and she said it should be dealt with severely. She used the word *broken*—the *broken* child, she'd say, the child would *never be normal*, the child was *broken*—and I wanted to tell her that it wasn't a nice thing to say about anyone, especially a kid, but on the other hand I really liked Henrietta's manner when she said it. She became clearer, in a way, and I'd gone with her up to Mark's.

He lived in a small one-bedroom flat on the edge of town, and he had a girlfriend whose name was Majken but whom everyone called the Switchman's Shanty, because that's what Mark called her. She was such a desperate type, Henrietta said, riding the bus in from the country every day, but when we got there it was the would-be teacher who opened the door, and when Henrietta asked for Mark, he said that Mark would be out in a little while, we could just have a seat, and so we did. I sat and wondered how long we'd be sitting there, and then Mark emerged from the bedroom. He came out and said that he'd just popped into the Switchman's Shanty, "And now I'm all yours." Then they laughed, Henrietta and the would-be teacher, and the Switchman's Shanty also laughed when she appeared a little while later.

I didn't know if I ought to laugh too, or how long we were supposed to remain seated, and since this was after the business in the cafeteria, I really shouldn't have been sitting there at all. But then we were drinking beer, and I could tell it would be only a matter of time before the wind shifted. And then here it came: "Mette," I heard, as Mark went over to a wall where he'd hung up a bunch of curios from a trip to Morocco. "Mette," he said, taking down an oblong object a good yard in length. It looked like beef jerky, and he threw it in my lap and asked if I knew what it was. "Yeah," I said, "it's a dried bull pizzle," and then Henrietta howled with laughter. The would-be teacher laughed too, and the Switchman's Shanty was apparently out in the kitchen, but Mark's eyes grew still. Still, but not frozen. More like one of those places that leases farm machinery, after closing time—the plowshares, the leaking grease fittings. Then he said that he hadn't reckoned I'd know. "Nice job," he said, and hung the pizzle back up on the wall, while Henrietta laughed so hard that she almost couldn't get it under control. I looked parched in my face, she said. "You look simply withered, Mette." A little while later I wanted to go home, and then the Switchman's Shanty wanted to go home too. We walked to the station together, and I remember her telling me how funny Mark was when they were alone. He was a real teddy bear, she said, breaking twigs off the hedges we passed. I thought of Henrietta, her laughter, I thought of the would-be teacher, his unmoving features, and what sort of person brings a pizzle home from holiday. That isn't normal, I thought, and then it was right after New Year's and we were headed to England, and on board the ferry Mark told me about the freezer chest.

He told me that he'd been a good guitarist once. "Do you believe me?" he asked, and I could tell I was supposed to say yes. I didn't actually care, but there was a mood around the table that expected me to say yes and so I said yes. We would be in London for a week, I was already feeling homesick, and Henrietta was sitting next to me, so I said that yes, I believed he'd been talented on the guitar. Mark smiled, and I smiled, and he smiled back at me, and I thought how much easier it was this way. For all I cared he could have been a virtuoso. He could have been Eric Clapton or someone. It didn't matter. What mattered were the others, and I thought I needed to leave it open. I had to allow him inside, even though one time, out in the hallway by our classroom, Mark had said, "Mette isn't chubby, she's fat," so that everyone could hear. Henrietta had been there that day too, Henrietta and the would-be teacher, but sometimes you have to eat shit, I thought, and said, "Yes, I believe you when you say you were a talented guitarist." I said it so that everyone could hear, and then he got to the freezer chest.

He said that unfortunately, he'd been robbed of his great talent, because one day he'd been rummaging around in his grandmother's freezer chest, whose hinge mechanism turned out to be broken, and just as he was standing there about to grab some cinnamon kringles, the freezer lid had slammed down on his fingers. The freezer chest had crushed them. "See for yourself," he said, waving his stumpy fingers in my face. "See, I'll never barre a chord again." There was a silence, Henrietta smiled, and I said, "That's really a shame," and he said, "You think so?" "Yes," I said, "I do think so," and then he paused deliberately, before saying, "But it's all just bullshit, you little fool." He said it easily, and then our corner dipped as the ferry to England hit a wave, and Henrietta, with her special insight into evil, could barely keep her seat.

It was as if a heavy lid had slammed shut within me. That's how I recall it, a great lid, and beneath it a frozen darkness that was all my own. While Mark held forth on my naïveté for the others, I fell back into the dark and thought of things that were impervious—cement floors, plexiglass, ice packs—and that the safest way to avoid people like Mark was to seal yourself off, and then, when you were sealed off, it was about your face and getting it back in position, getting it to close over the darkness and everything you have stored inside. So when he raised his beer with the others, I said that if he thought I was so dumb we could make a bet about who'd score highest on the graduating exams, and he said, "Sure, no problem," and I said, "All right then, no problem," and he laughed, saying, "Fuck yeah," and I got to my feet, and he said we'd bet a pizza, and I said, "No problem." He wanted to shake on it. I slapped my hand against his chubby outstretched fingers and walked straight out onto the deck, and I'd like to think I stared out toward England. It was in any case ocean that I stared out over, and there isn't much more to say about that week in London other than that I spent a week in London when I was eighteen.

It wasn't very hard to do better on the finals than Mark. I just got up every day and took care of my schoolwork and took care of myself. I also let Henrietta think what she wanted to whenever she said that if you compared the story about the freezer chest to something like incest, I was being hypersensitive, and then she'd look self-important, while one month led to the next and in June we graduated. I got the second highest marks in the school, while Mark did well enough that he was going to go to teachers college. Henrietta told me that as we rode around on the back of the decorated flatbed truck from one set of parents to the next, little Danish flags waving in the wind, most of us drunk from all the drinks they served us, and it was at one of those receptions, when everyone had had enough and someone finally turned down the stereo, that Mark came over to me.

He tapped me on the shoulder and said that a man was a man and that he was a twit. He wanted to admit that he'd lost our bet. I'd actually gone and done really well on the finals, he said. I didn't say anything, but somebody clapped, and he said, "There was something about a pizza, wasn't there?" and I said, "No." And he said, "Yes there was," that he wanted to spring for a pizza, and I said I didn't want a pizza. "Yes of course you do," Henrietta said, but I didn't want a pizza. "You can take your pizza and stick it up sideways," I said, and I said it so everyone could hear, for at that point I'd already found the room in Copenhagen, university lay ahead and Jutland behind, so fuck what they thought. It got quiet. Mark said that well, if that was the way I felt about it. "That's the way I feel about it," I said, and Henrietta said, "Now stop it, Mette, of course that's not the way you feel," and Mark said that I was obviously bearing a grudge, and Henrietta said it was embarrassing, and Mark said something about small minds, and Poul said well he'd be happy to eat a pizza, and Starling turned the stereo back up, while somewhere on the periphery our English teacher put his glasses on. I placed my hands on my knees and gazed at them, my fingers had glossy nails, blue by the cuticle, and what I remember most after Mark left was Henrietta leaning over me. "Shame on you," she said, and I'd like to know if she ever did anything about it, the incest.

MANITOBA

THERE'S A FAINT GLOW BEHIND THE MAPLE, BUT IT'S probably no one. The road is wet, drizzle, they're sleeping now. It's one in the morning, and he can see his face indistinctly in the living room window. They came last week, pitched camp across the road, pup tents and a large common tent. They're fourteen or fifteen, and they've brought leaders with them. But late in the evening they run around on the road, or they stand over there and scream. It's high summer. He can hear everything; it's the neighbor's field. The neighbor owns the ground down to the river and insists on his property rights. "It'll be nice with some youngsters," the farmer's wife said when she stood in his hall and briefed him on their coming.

They showed up on the sixteenth of July and set up their tents in a pattern that appeared deliberate. He stood on the corner of his lot and observed the little society take shape. The youth stand in knots between the tents and jostle each other. They shout when they walk to and from the portajohns. He has the sense that the village regards them as a miracle, but the miracle is noisy. When it's time for it to sleep, it runs around on the dirt roads, it hides in the bushes and undergrowth. It stands about rooting around in its mouth on the path to the school and whispering in the light of smartphones. Already on the second evening, he stood in the dark and listened to their animal sounds. Their shrieking echoed among the farmer's pig barns, and they didn't stop making noise till almost eleven. Then he stood on the edge of the field and watched the light from their phones flickering in the tents.

There's a place out on the flats, a small cabin. The summer deer season's over, he could go out there. It's a hunting cabin, no doubt, but he doesn't know whose, and the locals insist on their property rights. They don't understand that he's alone either. It's a pity he can't find someone, they think. But the person that you pity is a person in your power. He knows that, and now they're screaming. Other people's kids, teenagers. One of them appeared in his driveway the night before last. He was standing up by the garage when the kid, a girl, turned up with her head tilted to one side. "Who are you?" she asked, to show she was brave enough to be impudent. He could easily have answered, but he didn't. Then she kicked the gravel, disappeared.

He isn't being overrun, but it's hard nevertheless to keep people away from his door. In the beginning, when he was first living here, a woman with a little dog would come by now and then. She'd find some pretext to stop in front of the house. Mona, she was called. She came by with peeled windfall apples and recipes for venison. Once he gave her a cup of coffee in the kitchen. She said he had a nice place and examined the walls for portraits. Then she said there was a community dinner the following Thursday, and would he come? He couldn't, he said.

That wasn't true. He could have, but he didn't want to. Even during his short marriage, his eyes were usually fixed on the door to the office. He corrected essays in there, or watched the traffic down on Tagensvej. The young people biking to and from school, their thin hair rustling under knit caps. It was nice to sit there and watch them from above, and once in a while over the years there would be a girl in his class, one of those with potential. She would make something out of her essays. Often she'd be standing nearby when he came out of the teacher's lounge. Her eyes would be large with questions, and in the end she'd vanish. Now there are scouts across the road, but out on the flats there's a hunting cabin. It says MANITOBA in black paint on a length of driftwood, up on the gable. Two mugs have been set on the windowsill, a teaspoon in each. So two people sit out there at regular intervals. They sit and watch the roe deer, the foxes. If it were him sitting out there, he'd be relishing the fact that you can always withdraw a little bit further.

When that woman, Mona, was in the house, she said, "But then your kids must be in Copenhagen, right?" He didn't owe her an answer. Her children were spread out, but they were grown now, she said. She took the dog on walks, of course, and now he's got the sense that people pity him. There's nothing to pity, even if it cost him the marriage. But a divorced man who isn't being looked after is a man in free fall, plunging into a swamp of his own making. That's how they see it, so he keeps the gravel and the driveway tidy. Each morning, he raises the blinds. The young farmworkers who live around town never think to raise their blinds. That's a woman's job. It isn't until the farmworkers get a girlfriend that the blinds go up. But he raises his own blinds, so he's probably gay. He used to be a teacher and have to deal with other people's kids. And that's what he did, until she was standing there with her lunchbox. It was during lunch hour, by the bike shed. For a long time he drove a Lada, but then he switched to a bike. She stood quietly next to his luggage rack. From a distance it looked as if she wanted to ask about an assignment. Up close, the skin of her face was thin and alive.

Enough already, but they're screaming, and he wishes he were sitting in Manitoba. If he were, he would wait for sunrise, lens trained on the reedbed. This spring the bittern sounded like a foghorn in the landscape. As if it knew everything. It would have been easier if he'd been a widower, he thinks, because then an aversion to death might keep them from his door, and there's a glow over by the maple, behind the birdbath. Maybe there's someone there. He's not sure, but in the reflection from the living room window he resembles a normal man around sixty. He no longer has any wish to regulate his abnormalities, only to withdraw. If he walks southwest, he'll have to cross a couple of drainage channels and a fen with beef cattle to reach Manitoba. He could take a sleeping bag, he thinks. If he's caught sleeping in another man's hunting cabin, he'll have to put his house up for sale. Maybe that would be for the best. He should have bought a place at the end of a dirt road after all. They do agree on everything here. Property rights are holy, youth is a virtue, and the wolf that's been sighted in the tree plantation should be shot. It's only a question of time before it gets together with another wolf, has pups, and forms a pack. It's happened other places and it'll happen here too. They won't stand for it. His neighbor's got a Small Munsterlander. They walk around, out in the plantation, and look for the wolf. He's got a deer stand out there. Then he can watch the animals from a slightly elevated perspective. His wife isn't afraid of the wolf; there isn't anything she's afraid of. Yet she dislikes disorder, and now they're providing the ground for a summer camp on their fallow field. The field stretches down to the river. During the day, the young people build rafts and towers from spruce poles. The other morning they woke the village with song. "Isn't it lovely having some youngsters around?" asked the farmer and his wife afterward. "Yes," he replied, "but they scream in the evening." The farmer and his wife couldn't hear them, they said, pointing at the farmhouse. It sat right behind the tent area. "They scream like wild animals," he said, and now there's that glow beneath the maple again. It's by the birdbath, a figure. And now he can see her, a girl scout in the summer darkness with fever-white hair. He's turned everything off in the living room, and she probably can't see him. Her face takes on an odd luminosity from her phone. He can see her chewing her lip in concentration. Now she raises her eyes. It's the girl from the driveway. She peers at the window, eyes wide. Quickly he shoves his face against the pane, pressing, opening his mouth. His teeth touch glass and her throat muscles tense, then she bolts like an animal down the bank, across the road, in her nightshirt.

At the moment there's no hunting. They've just finished shooting the summer roebucks. He can walk wherever he wants, across the fen, along the thickets, over the flats with a sleeping pad. "Don't expect to come here and change anything," they told him when he moved in. Some good advice, they thought. "That's really not my intention," he replied, indicating his adaptability with a smile. He has a flashlight out by the fuse box. He goes out and puts it in his backpack. In the kitchen he turns the electric kettle on. He should have said that they shouldn't expect to change him either, but that's not how the song goes, and he grabs a screwdriver. The door to Manitoba is undoubtedly locked.

WILD SWIMS

IN THE EVENING, THE HEAT HUNG HEAVY IN THE APART-
ment. I sat down on the floor in my underwear, closed my
eyes. Down on the street the ambulances drove to and fro,
but I've learned not to chase sirens anymore. As I sat there, I
visualized a vast chilly landscape. It was soothing for a while,
but after midnight everything was sticking to me. I went for a
walk, out toward the big houses around Carlsberg. The front
yards there smelled of elder and peony, and it's good to walk
at night. I thought of Emilie as I looked at the sleeping houses.
As kids we wore dresses with goldfish and pleaded for candy
and kittens. I thought of the neighbor's cattle back home,
the brick transformer tower, the fjord, and in the direction
of Vesterbro I kept hearing sirens.

The next day I decided to bike to the beach, but instead I
went out to Kastellet. I walked slowly around the fort, looking at the flowers and the water in the moat. It has its own
geography, the water, and certain places were choked with
duckweed. I saw swans and ducklings in the grass, while the
coots grew agitated among the water lilies. It was a muted life.
A swan flew across the scene, then a helicopter, then a couple
of ducks, then another helicopter. The sky arched overhead,
the geese grazed, and it wasn't that the idyll was getting to
be too much; it was more that it was there yet had vanished
anyway, and then I was on the cusp of tears.

On my way out I read the sign with the commandant's regulations. It didn't say anything about not swimming in the moat. Once in a while somebody must jump in, I thought. Wild swims are becoming increasingly popular across Europe. I've heard of a British woman, for instance, who managed to swim her way up through a large lake system somewhere in the middle of England. Every midsummer night she was out swimming, and I imagine her fighting her way up salmon ladders and into still waters.

Once when we were little, Emilie and I, we gripped each other's hand and waded out by Pigsfoot Spit. We ventured one step at a time and took turns leading. First Emilie wanted to turn around, then I did, then I got scared of the crabs, then she did. We squealed with delight and terror, until suddenly we stood on the edge of the old channel, a tar-black river of crabs and slime. Our feet had never seemed so white before. Emilie's like snow, and my right foot with the birthmark; one step and we'd sink into the darkness. It was Emilie who tried to step away first. She tugged on me, and if she hadn't, where would I have ended up? Someplace in the North Sea—Flat Grounds? Dogger Bank? Somewhere else, in any case, than where we are now, far from each other.

It had been a knifing near Central Station, my downstairs neighbor said. A prostitute, probably. But the next night the ambulances were out again, and the heat kept me awake. I sat down on the floor across from the fridge. Nothing's static, certainly not me, I thought. Then you've got to live. Then you've got to die. That's the way it is, but it's strange to imagine your own death, so I tried to picture Mom and Dad's kitchen instead. The vinyl floor, the stove hood, the grandkids' drawings. The wedding photo of my brother and his wife, she in white, he in something resembling an iron lung. Sunday afternoon in the country, and when I shut my eyes, what I saw was a distant relative, head down in the freezer chest, hunting for kringles.

Nothing moved. Each time my skin touched another part of my skin, it stuck. If I were still the same as when I was nineteen, I'd bike out to Kastellet right now and go swimming, I thought, and opened the fridge, pulled out the crisper drawer, and stuck my feet in instead.

The next morning I had an urge to go to the swimming pool. The last time I'd been to one, Emilie was there too, so it must have been elementary school. "Then it's high time you went," I told myself, yet even before I reached my bike, down in the courtyard, I was regretting my decision and didn't want to go through with it. The alternative was to give up, and that's one way we're *not* alike, Emilie and I. I give up only reluctantly.

Sitting in front of the pool building were two guys from the local drunkards' bench. The one was fanning himself with a voucher from the city, the other scratching his skinny neck. They each had a beer in hand, and I could see they'd been in the showers, but also that their hair shone in the sun with a water-repellent sheen. "They never fix the sauna," one of them said as I locked my bike, "but every time some schoolkid shits the pool, they shut everything down. Last week a little brown turd was swimming around down in the deep end. So they drained everything." I stood still, leaning over my luggage rack. "They've changed the water, darling," the skinny one said. "And you needn't worry about us. We never get as far as the pool."

It was too late to turn back now, and in the long run it was cheapest to buy a ten-visit card, said the girl in the glass cage. So that's what I did, and when I'd done that, I found the changing room full of women and scratched lockers. I can't start anything I can't finish. If I don't finish it I feel weak, and if I feel weak, it just spreads. I rooted around in my wallet, my pockets, the bottom of my bag for a ten-krone coin for the locker.

"Need change?" asked a woman's voice. She looked like she might have been from India. "I'm not used to using the pool," I said, and she said, "If you've got a twenty," and she jingled two ten-krone pieces in her palm. We traded, and I didn't know where to look while she took off her clothes. I started by removing my shoes, then my T-shirt, my skirt, and though I rarely fold my clothes properly otherwise, I creased and smoothed till I stood looking down at myself and thought, there you have me: Flat Grounds.

I found a shower diagonally across from her. An older woman was scrubbing her body as if it were a plank floor. Meanwhile, the Indian woman had her own special system for washing herself: hands, feet, face. There was something ceremonial about it, also when she donned her bathing cap, and two showers down stood a woman with a lady razor. She was trimming her pubes, and she passed the blades across her labia as though the razor were a bow and her pussy a violin. When she turned her backside to me I could see she was called Amy.

I wanted to go home, but I can't walk backwards. I remembered how we were on the way out by Pigsfoot Spit. Emilie with knock-knees, and I with the birthmark on my right foot, which now found itself over a shower grate at Vesterbro Indoor Pool, distant in time and space, and it surprised me that my birthmark was still there, and still looked like the island of Anholt seen from the air.

When the Indian woman put on her suit, I put on mine. When she walked out of the showers, I walked behind her. The door she opened, onto a set of stairs, I opened too. It was white and wet in the staircase, and it smelled of algae and chlorine. I walked a few steps behind the Indian woman, whose heels were cracked. She opened the door to the pool and I followed. She went calmly over to the lip of the shrieking water-hell, giving her bathing cap an extra downward tug. Then she stepped over to the ladder and started to climb down. When her body was ninety-five percent submerged in chlorine, she let herself be swallowed up. First she was a shadow in the water; then she popped up in lane three.

I don't like having my head underwater, so I walked over to lane four in the shallow end, eased myself gingerly into the pool, and swam out. I looked for feces in the water but didn't see any. I glanced over at the pool toys and the noisy children. I caught sight of a hairy man who was standing in the shallow end of lane one. He had a snorkel on and dived underwater every time a woman swam past. I wanted to do ten laps, then I wanted to go home. I thought about rivers with distant sources. I thought of the carp at Kastellet, the light down there in the deeps. I thought of the water lilies, the geese, and the heavy organic chill. I wanted to block out the channel and tried to swim with my eyes closed, but when I did, I drifted over into the Indian woman's lane.

On the seventh lap my hands hurt. Through the deep end of the pool, a beef-colored figure suddenly glided along the bottom. I missed a stroke, got water in my mouth. Tried to find my footing, but of course there was nothing beneath me. My head went under several times before I grabbed hold of one of the flexible lane markers. I used it to get myself over to the end of the lane, beneath a diving block. There my feet found a narrow ledge to stand upon. The figure was gliding along the bottom of the pool in the direction of the diving board. I stared until the surface of the water broke. First the top of a wet head. Then two small hard eyes with a wet mouth at the bottom.

I looked for the Indian woman, whose feet I saw disappearing up to the changing room. I clung to the edge of the pool and watched the beef-colored figure clamber out. I watched how, with his back to me, he rubbed himself briefly with a towel. Then he flung it over his shoulder and sauntered past above my head. White sodden trunks, half-stiff prick, swimming goggles. I've lost her, I thought, and glanced across the pool at the same instant the hairy man in the first lane dove because the woman with the shaved genitals was passing by, doing the crawl. And I looked down: my white feet on the narrow ledge, beneath me the deeps, clinical and descaled. Emilie's hand in mine. A step, the suction, and then off to other realms.

DORTHE NORS, one of the most original voices in contemporary Danish literature, was born in 1970 and holds a degree in literature and history from Aarhus University. She is the author of four novels, including *Mirror, Shoulder, Signal*, a finalist for the Man Booker International Prize; two novellas, collected in *So Much for That Winter*; and the story collection *Karate Chop*, winner of the Per Olov Enquist Literary Prize. Nors's short stories have appeared in numerous publications, including *Harper's Magazine*, *Tin House*, and *A Public Space*, and she is the first Danish writer ever to have a story published in the *New Yorker*. Nors lives in Denmark.

MISHA HOEKSTRA is an award-winning translator. He lives in Aarhus, where he writes and performs songs under the name Misha Hoist.

Book design and composition by Tetragon, London.
Manufactured by Versa Press on acid-free,
30 percent postconsumer wastepaper.